THE CARETAKER

THE
CARETAKER

Doon Arbus

A New Directions Book

First published clothbound by New Directions in 2020
Manufactured in the United States of America
Design by Erik Rieselbach

Library of Congress Cataloging-in-Publication Data
Names: Arbus, Doon, author.
Title: The caretaker / Doon Arbus.
Description: First edition. | New York : A New Directions Book, [2020]
Identifiers: LCCN 2020021803 | ISBN 9780811229494 (cloth ; acid-free paper) |
ISBN 9780811229500 (ebook)
Subjects: LCSH: Museums—Fiction.
Classification: LCC PS3601.R37 C37 2020 | DDC 813/.6—dc23
LC record available at https://lccn.loc.gov/2020021803

2 4 6 8 10 9 7 5 3 1

New Directions Books are published for James Laughlin
by New Directions Publishing Corporation
80 Eighth Avenue, New York 10011

THE CARETAKER

It was the last of its kind, saved from extinction, not by any intrinsic Darwinian attribute, but by the whims of chance. It had survived the sudden recent influx of bulldozers and cranes and construction crews that had done away with its original neighbors, leaving in their wake a motley assortment of competing ambitions: faceted tiers of glass in the shape of a defunct wedding cake reflecting fragments of cloud back at the sky, windowless concrete bunkers for exhibiting art, a rose-colored ziggurat, and a pair of leaning towers, as yet unoccupied. This bombastically revitalized environment imposed upon the lone survivor—an unprepossessing three-story red brick building—a look of baffled stoicism. In the absence of any noteworthy architectural feature to justify its continued existence in the face of all this change, it squatted there stubbornly on its bit of turf, a dwarfed, defiant anachronism.

At certain times of day, in certain bright or fading light—a wintry afternoon glare, or at dusk before the intrusion of the streetlights—the raised lettering on the brass plaque beside the front door was easily misread as ORGAN FOUNDATION, which is what the locals took to calling it. "Meet you across from the Organ," they'd say with the breezy nonchalance of the initiate. This nickname—conjuring up a medical lab harvesting body parts or an obsolete musical instrument factory—derived from the fact that the plaque's initial capital *M* had lost its sharp edges (possibly due to an error at the foundry or excessive polishing) and had begun to recede into the background, managing at times to achieve invisibility. The plaque's subtitle however identified the building as the home of THE SOCIETY FOR THE PRESERVATION OF THE LEGACY OF DR. CHARLES ALEXANDER MORGAN—a Morgan unrelated to, and not to be confused with, the renowned financier of the same name with his eponymous well-endowed uptown Library, although such confusion frequently occurred, invariably to the benefit of the former residence of Dr. Charles, about one third of whose visitors came because they had mistaken it for that other, more notable venue. This is not to say that Dr. Charles Morgan did not have his own legitimate coterie of devotees determined to compensate for his relative lack of fame by the intensity of their allegiance. Many of them, along with members of the Society and invited guests, meet at the Foundation twice a year to celebrate the anniversaries of their hero's birth (August 29) and death (January 11) with refreshments, readings, and spirited discussions.

Twice a day, six days a week, the caretaker conducts tours of the premises and its collections. If you happened to be curious enough to pay a visit on a Saturday morning, for instance—a Saturday similar to so many that have come and gone since the fall of 1989 when, with little fanfare, the Morgan Foundation declared itself open to the public—you might find other would-be visitors meandering down the block. They come singly; they come by twos or threes. Those venturing up the stoop will usually discover the front door slightly ajar, but since this seems less an invitation than an oversight, they hesitate for fear of trespassing. Peering inside does little to reassure them. They find no one there to greet them, just other uneasy, waiting visitors gathered in a makeshift vestibule, a room awkwardly truncated by the addition of a pair of mahogany sliding doors, currently closed.

The size of the group that assembles here—which, even in the Foundation's heyday just after Morgan's death, numbered less than twenty—has been steadily shrinking. There are still, from time to time, the small enclaves of foreign sightseers who speak scarcely any English but are nonetheless resigned to being led around and lectured to. There are the women, likely members of a cultural club on one of their regular excursions, helping themselves to the free leaflets on display. There is the occasional couple, young or not so young, hoping for an unorthodox romantic adventure, lured by the dim lighting and an anticipated atmosphere of reverence. There is the single parent with a reluctant teenager in tow; someone killing time between appointments in the neighborhood; the student doing research. Each new arrival is subjected by his predecessors to a surreptitious appraisal, a look verging on the xenophobic that seems to say: If *you* have chosen to come here, *I* must be in the wrong place.

By the time the caretaker makes his entrance—always punctual, never early—to rescue the room's occupants from themselves and one another, the waiting period has lulled them beyond impatience into resignation, a state just short of somnambulism, out of which the sliding doors' low reluctant groan startles them; they turn as one toward the sound. The figure in the doorway, an angular, somewhat off-kilter silhouette, greets them, cheerlessly, by rote. "Good morning all," he says, addressing no one in particular as he slides the doors shut behind him and proceeds to a table at the east wall.

He is a monochromatic man. Dust is his color. It envelops every aspect of his person, hair, skin, eyes, clothing, softening all distinctions. The furrows in his otherwise unspoiled face suggest an outdoor life, weathered by sun and wind, but his current pallor makes recent exposure to the elements unlikely. "Welcome to the home of Dr. Charles Alexander Morgan," he continues as he stations himself behind the table, absentmindedly realigning the cashbox, the stack of leaflets, and the portable

5

credit card processor; fingering a roll of red tickets (the generic kind, available in any stationery store), and the leather-bound horizontal ledger serving as a guestbook. "I'm the caretaker. I'm here to be your guide." He pauses and with a sigh, as if this next disclosure were more a confession than a point of information, introduces himself by name.

Once the preliminaries have been dispensed with (admission fees in exchange for tickets—cash preferred, exact change if possible—and the ritual signing of the guestbook, address required, to facilitate future solicitation of funds), the caretaker will slide the door open once again and lead the way into the room beyond, pausing on the other side to supervise entry. One by one, as demanded by his staging, members of the group pass single file through the opening. They sidle past him obediently, heads lowered, as he stands to one side, rhythmically clicking the counter in his left hand, totting up the numbers (6, 7, 8 ...) to check and recheck as they move through the house, lest someone linger behind, disobeying the rules, secreting themselves in a dark corner, touching or rearranging the treasures of the place, or, worse still, pocketing something small. As they commence the tour, visitors find themselves in a wide windowless hallway, its walls adorned from floor to ceiling with an eclectic mass of artifacts, punctuated by the occasional glass cabinet, spotlit from above to theatrical effect, which nonetheless does little to improve the visibility of its contents. A long waist-level double-sided vitrine bisects the room, making navigation difficult.

At first glance the display looks not so much haphazard as deliberately organized to confound comprehension. Ordinary domestic items (a wire hanger, a chewing-gum wrapper, locks with and without their keys, a broken hinge, a watch without a watchband, a toilet plunger, a plastic coffee lid) vie for position with a smattering of gilt-framed eighteenth-century oil portraits, a large multifaceted jewel, an African mask of teak and straw, a pair of pearl-handled dueling pistols aimed at one another. Nature has its place here, too: seashells, dried leaves, driftwood, lumps of coal, a human skull. Objects are fastened to the walls or occupy small specially designed shelves. It is almost possible to decipher the small numbers stenciled near each item, suggesting some sort of identification system. With no instruction, the newcomers begin to reassemble themselves shoulder to shoulder as if by instinct just inside the room, forming a squashed horseshoe. All along the dark plank floor, at a distance from the walls of about a foot, a strip of black tape symbolizes a barrier, the only obstacle between the curious and the many tantalizingly unprotected things confronting them. Some crane their necks to see. Others bend forward precariously, hands on knees. There is usually at least one unwitting transgressor, who obliges the caretaker to remonstrate.

"Keep your distance, please," he warns in an undertone all the more imposing for its lack of volume. "Mind the barrier. Touching is forbidden."

If you were raised on the classics and have come to believe in fate, you might say that the caretaker's fate embraced him twenty-five years earlier on a chilly winter evening in a rooming house in Prague when, bending over a stack of discarded English-language newspapers waiting to be crumpled into fuel, he chanced upon the following headline: *Dr. Charles A. Morgan, Chemist, Author, Philosopher & Collector, Dies at 66.* As the caretaker later recounted the event to the hiring committee, he fixated on these words for several minutes, reading and rereading them in a futile attempt to amend the stated facts. News of the death of an intimate could not have been more shattering to his sense of equilibrium. In his student days, he had encountered his intellectual lodestar in Morgan's seminal volume, *Stuff*, an experience that marked him forever. He discovered in the book many of his own inchoate thoughts expressed in the words of a kindred spirit. In fact, such an affinity existed between the writer's psyche and his own that it often seemed as if a sentence on the page and its echo in his mind had sprung into being simultaneously, leaving him incapable of distinguishing the conjurer from the conjured. The book had become, in a sense, his bible; it accompanied him everywhere. Although his relationship to its author was, of course, entirely one-sided, it remained nonetheless solely responsible for his feeling less alone in the world.

After recovering from his initial shock at the news—which was at that point over four months old—he continued reading. The obituary went on to pronounce its subject "the last renaissance man of his generation," a tribute hovering deliberately somewhere between praise and condemnation, qualified in advance (as superlatives usually are in responsible publications) by a one-word disclaimer ("arguably") that rendered the statement toothless. It reported that while on an expedition to Karachi in pursuit of a coveted artifact for his collection, Dr. Morgan—who was said to have been in excellent health—had collapsed on a crowded sidewalk and been rushed to a local hospital, where he died within hours, a ruptured brain aneurysm cited as the cause.

In the established style of such announcements, a description of the deceased followed: "Although small in stature, Dr. Morgan was a formidable presence, with a leonine head of white hair and the scrupulously maintained muscular physique of a one-time amateur boxer. A millionaire (self-made, unmade, and made again) in an era when the word was still synonymous with extreme wealth, his attendance at a social gathering or a cultural event, where he could be found sporting one of his distinctive custom-made three-piece English suits and colorful tie, surrounded by admirers, was in and of itself enough to sanction the event's importance. Thanks to his virtually insatiable curiosity about almost any topic, he proved to be a discerning listener as well as a celebrated raconteur with an inexhaustible repertoire of stories. His refusal to mince words, however, often left even his most loyal colleagues and closest friends disenchanted. Few had managed to escape the sting of his mordant wit. Although unabashed in the pursuit of his various passions, Dr. Morgan nonetheless simultaneously continued performing his many anonymous acts of spontaneous philanthropy."

The next three paragraphs summarized Morgan's life; a fourth debated the relative importance of his achievements in various fields, enumerating the awards he'd won in each capacity, and supporting each opinion with carefully selected quotations from colleagues and critics. It suggested that, although any attempt to assess the ultimate significance of the Morgan collection would probably be premature at this stage, the influence of *Stuff*, his book on the subject—subtitled "A Meditation on the Charisma of Things"—would be "impossible to exaggerate": political theorists had embraced his "disquisition on individuality and its dependence on the group for context" as a philosophical underpinning of democracy; libraries and museums had revised their cataloging systems in accordance with his new typological principles; psychologists had coined the word "Morganism" to identify the neurotic fear of insubstantiality afflicting the obsessive collector. Finally, to sum matters up, the obituary stated that Dr. Morgan, being childless, with no siblings, and parents long since dead, "is survived by his wife of forty-three years, the former Helen Clay, who has been appointed director of the Society for the Preservation of the Legacy of Dr. Charles Morgan and president of his Foundation."

Within a month of perusing these facts, the man destined to become caretaker of the Foundation had mailed to Morgan's widow, in care of the Foundation, a personal letter two pages long, with his handwritten résumé enclosed, offering his services in any capacity she might determine he could be of use.

Despite having remained his wife in name and status (dutifully performing the role long enough to become his widow), many years had passed since Mrs. Morgan, the former Helen Clay, had actually lived with the man she called her husband. Encouraged by her physicians, she had removed herself from the premises decades earlier, finding the three-story building itself—not to mention its primary resident, presiding over it as both his private museum and his home—too cold and demanding for someone in her delicate physical condition to endure. Her multiple ailments, if not life-threatening, proved to be chronically debilitating, despite the absence of satisfactory diagnoses. "A cracked pot never breaks," Morgan was fond of saying whenever his wife invoked her beleaguered health as an intimation of imminent mortality, adding as reassurance that he was certain to predecease her. In the early stages of their physical and psychic schism, the couple had agreed that a divorce would be both unnecessary and politically unwise, so they continued to function as a unit in their areas of mutual influence, providing each other with companionship in public and, on rare occasions, in private as well.

Dr. Morgan, being no fool, had of course resigned himself to the fact that he—like everyone else, including others similarly convinced of their own greatness—would eventually die. In recognition of this lamentable inevitability, he had set about attempting to ensure that his posthumous existence—what you might call, in a purely practical sense, his afterlife—would conform as strictly as possible to his vision of it. In short, about three years before his death, he made a Will.

The attorney, who drew up the twenty-four-page document, and in whose safe it resided until Morgan's death, was reputed to be the most prominent practitioner in his specialized field of expertise, boasting a glittering clientele (both living and dead) of celebrities, artists, financiers, and power mongers, whose concerns for their own mortality had propelled his career. Morgan's Last Will and Testament—with its requisite boilerplate, its seven sonorous prefatory *Whereases*, its multiple *Articles* and *Recitations*, its subtended *Schedules* and *Appendices*—made the usual futile attempt to mount on behalf of the deceased's wishes an impenetrable defense against whatever unforeseen assaults the future would inevitably bring. Even a cursory reading of the Will revealed where Dr. Morgan's allegiances lay, demonstrating that he cared more for the fate of his building and its contents—to which he had devoted himself for nearly half a century—than for any living creature. Aside from certain specific bequests to his wife, to a few friends, and to fewer charities, the bulk of his estate endowed in perpetuity his Foundation, the Society, and the preservation of his collection as a private museum.

Although he died unexpectedly, alone and far from home among strangers whose language he neither spoke nor understood, Dr. Morgan died prepared. In choosing his wife to preside over his legacy, he had chosen well. His death had an immediate salutary effect upon his new widow's regard and affection for him, reviving in her feelings that had been quashed by her exposure to the harsh daily realities of his nature. As a memory, he achieved absolution in her eyes. The metamorphosis enabled her to forgive his transgressions and to regard even his most abrasive habits as mere harmless eccentricities. His absence healed the rift.

Wearing her widowhood proudly and seeking to wield her power as his anointed primary representative on earth, she set about interpreting his desires, both expressed and unexpressed, concerning everything he had left behind. When it came to the building and its contents, it was she who insisted that the objects to be enshrined were not limited to the items in Morgan's collection, but included anything he might have touched, worn, used, sat upon, or gazed at before leaving home for the last time. In this regard, she found herself at odds with several of the other six Board members appointed by Morgan in his Will, who lodged objections both practical and philosophical: they protested that treating Morgan's personal commonplaces with the same reverence accorded the collection's artifacts would be to make a mockery of his life's work; they argued that doing so would place an additional, unwarranted burden on the endowment funds.

Pending the resolution of these and other related machinations, the manila envelope postmarked Prague and addressed in a cramped, studied penmanship to *Mrs. Charles (Helen) Morgan* had lain unopened for weeks in the widow's inbox at the Foundation, along with other accumulating mail. By the time the Board issued its press release announcing late September as the scheduled opening date of the Morgan Foundation, only four months remained in which to hire and train the required staff to deal with both the daunting conservation issues and the anticipated influx of visiting public. No ads had been placed, no applicants had as yet come forward when the widow finally turned her attention to the waiting envelope. In the absence of any other candidates for the position of caretaker, she viewed its contents as a singularly providential, if unsolicited, application for the job and, as such, enthusiastically shared the letter and accompanying résumé with the Board, which responded with skepticism.

Everyone admitted that the letter itself contained some well-chosen phrases, demonstrating—as far as was possible in a two-page note from a stranger to a recent widow—a commendable sensitivity to the recipient's state of mind, while simultaneously conveying an appreciation of the intentions and achievements of her husband's work that wisely stopped short of idolatry. The writer had begun by apologizing for intruding on the widow's "unimaginable solitary grief" by succumbing to a selfish need to express to someone close to the deceased his own "singular desolation over the loss." He spoke of "a first encounter with the uncompromising mind of Dr. Morgan" and its transformational effect on the rest of his life, calling the experience "a revelation" that had forced him to recognize the indispensable value of classification to anyone committed to the pursuit of meaning. He said that, "in memory of such a man," he would be "proud to be of service in any capacity."

But while most Board members found the letter impressive enough, the résumé left them troubled. If acquisitiveness in some form had been Morgan's weakness, the individual currently under consideration was his antipode. The résumé they were in the process of considering inadvertently detailed a downward trajectory from success toward failure, from achievement toward renunciation, a process of divestiture that bore a disconcerting resemblance to flight. The virtues it encapsulated included a wide spectrum of experience in varied fields of endeavor, but the experiences were disconcertingly brief—a disjointed series of aborted beginnings—as if intended to fend off progress. Although the candidate had undoubtedly showed considerable promise in his youth, the diversity of his gifts nullified one another, inhibiting his ability to excel at anything.

While still a boy he had won a coveted music scholarship on the basis of his talent as a pianist but after a single semester had withdrawn from the program and thereupon abandoned the instrument forever. His innate physical grace (which he bore almost as an affliction and took great pains to conceal) proved useless in the realm of competitive sports since he lacked the competitive spirit. In college, while majoring in Art, he gained some recognition as a draftsman in the eyes of his professors and, with their help and encouragement, managed to get his work included in a few local group exhibitions where it garnered a modicum of critical praise, but in the end his facility at rendering made him lazy and contemptuous of his own accomplishments. He was a good mimic and extemporaneous speaker and enjoyed momentary stardom as a member of the debating team until one night when he suddenly suffered a failure of nerve and became inarticulate. He might eventually have turned into a proficient poet had he not condemned his initial efforts as derivative and all those who failed to perceive their obvious flaws as ignorant or lacking in discrimination. History intrigued him, although he remained constantly suspicious of the alleged facts, and only managed to pursue it as a study of rumors, lies, and competing fictions. The Physical Sciences, with their promise of provable theorems, attracted him more, chemistry and physiology in particular. His natural fascination with how things worked made him a tireless, even obsessive, researcher, but once satisfied that he'd grasped an animating mechanism, his interest promptly evaporated and he succumbed to the first available distraction. Over and over again, the drone in his nature saved him, but idealism continued to be an obstacle.

Toward the end of his senior year of college, after being accepted to medical school (envisioning a modest future as a hospital pathologist) he came upon the work of Dr. Charles Alexander Morgan, which revolutionized his thinking, spurring him to change course and opt for graduate school instead. Morgan's book, with its method for deciphering hidden relationships between things in a world apparently bereft of meaning, offered him a lifeline; he declared himself a disciple. The book did not, however, cure his restive spirit. His doctoral thesis—in which Dr. Morgan's work as chemist and theoretician was to have played a marginal role—remained less than halfway to completion when, hungering for a taste of the real world, he temporarily abandoned it to enlist for a two-year stint in the navy. It was peacetime, though; he saw no action. As it turned out, the intended hiatus never ended. Whether he was driven by a fear of failure, or by a lack of ambition, or a confidence in his own superiority that no actual achievement could ever match, at the conclusion of his military service and in the grand tradition of self-exiles, he began hiring himself out as an English teacher in countries whose languages he scarcely knew. The period customarily intended to enable a young person to find his way had, paradoxically, caused this particular one to lose his.

At this juncture in his life, just shy of middle age, he had visited more than a dozen different countries and found employment in nearly all of them. He had picked up a smattering of words and phrases in as many languages—from the bare essentials to the epithets and handy colloquialisms embraced by expatriates—and managed to feign a bit of fluency in two or three. He had lived and worked at home and abroad in noisy, overcrowded cities both exotic and mundane, in barren sparsely populated rural wastelands, and small towns. In addition to teaching English to foreign students overseas, he had been—though not necessarily in this order—a truck driver, a clerk in a second-hand bookstore, a deckhand on a ferry, a mortuary attendant, a gardener, a typesetter at a printing plant, a short order cook, a groom at a riding academy, an assistant librarian, a handyman, a gas station attendant, a telephone lineman, a lab technician, a tree surgeon, an encyclopedia salesman, part of a construction crew, a bartender, a farmhand, a writer for the English language newspaper in Athens, and currently for one in Prague.

Had he been wiser in the ways of the world or more sensitive to the concerns of a prospective employer, he would probably have omitted the majority of these experiences, colorful though they may have been, from his résumé. Such a checkered history, quite desirable in a dinner guest, could hardly have been so in a potential employee whose qualifications might logically be expected to include not only certain specialized skills but a high degree of loyalty, dependability, and dedication: in and of themselves, his former jobs, in their sheer number and variety, threatened to disqualify him for the position.

Once again, the widow and the Board members found themselves on opposite sides, and once again the majority acceded to her wishes in an effort to simulate common ground. In spite of their reservations, they issued the applicant an invitation—regarding it as a challenge in disguise—to present himself in three weeks at the Foundation at an appointed hour for a formal interview, and promised a prompt decision. It was a long way to go for a job interview and they were probably hoping he would not show up, but for a man so accustomed to turning his back on the present in favor of an unknown future, the possibility of professionally allying himself with a figure he held in such esteem must have struck him as well worth the risk. He wrote in reply that they should expect him. In the interim, the Board set about meeting with other candidates for the position, but the widow successfully vetoed every choice in anticipation of the first applicant's upcoming interview.

On a rainy, windy afternoon in early August, at the appointed hour of the appointed day, a bedraggled man in a dripping Macintosh and wide-brimmed leather hat presented himself on the Morgan Foundation's doorstep for his examination. He paused there and leaned forward, studying the inscription on the shiny brass plaque beside the entrance, touching the raised letters, tracing the shapes with his finger in a kind of benediction before pressing the buzzer. Moments later the intercom erupted with some bursts of static in answer to which he ventured what he imagined to be the desired reply by offering his name and adding, "I'm here for the interview," with an inflection that made a question of it. The door unlocked with a click, admitting him. Once across the threshold, having shut the door behind him, he removed his hat, laid down the satchel he'd been sheltering under his coat, and shook himself like a drenched dog before looking around to get his bearings.

The newly installed sliding doors stood wide open, affording a largely unobstructed view of the dim interior that extended to the rear of the building some hundred feet away. All at once, as if awakened by his arrival, lights came on in the far room. Someone was striding forward to greet him, a powerful-looking young man with a blond crew cut—savagely trimmed, as if the mere existence of hair betrayed a lack of discipline that had to be expunged—and the brusque, vaguely threatening aspect of a bouncer or a bodyguard, who introduced himself as Mrs. Morgan's special assistant. "They're ready for you. You can leave your wet things here," he said, gesturing toward an old-fashioned wooden coat tree by the front door. The visitor did as he was told, while his escort watched, making no move to assist. "Right this way," he said at last, jerking his head in the direction from which he'd come. "Follow me. It's upstairs." He led the way with the visitor trailing behind, holding the satchel against his chest, marveling at his surroundings and emitting the occasional odd, inadvertent gasp or groan of appreciation as he went. He did not get far before curiosity overwhelmed obedience.

He had fixated on a framed portrait of a woman, her half-averted face rendered in shades of black against a background of green paper, that hung on the wall about a foot higher than the top of his head amid a cluster of various small household objects. "Might I have just a moment, please," he said, and without waiting for a reply, drew a pair of glasses from the breast pocket of his jacket, positioned them just above the tip of his nose, and approached the picture, craning his neck to make out the details in the half light. Although the woman's face was depicted as only fractionally more than a profile, her wry, ineluctable, sidelong gaze managed to fix itself on the viewer, permitting no escape, regardless of how he might shift his position to avoid it. The visitor almost smiled. "Ah, the Dürer," he murmured under his breath. He would have lingered longer, but his escort had returned to his side to say, "Come on, we mustn't keep them waiting," and, bringing up the rear, no longer trusting his charge to follow, ushered him along, as if shooing away a pigeon.

In this reconfigured formation, they headed up the staircase. Here, too, the wall was encrusted with things to admire, although in contrast to the first installation, which accentuated dissonance, these objects were grouped thematically, some half-dozen to a set: writing implements, pinioned horseflies, door-knockers, wishbones, a cluster of daguerreotypes. The visitor, conscious of the impatient man at his heels, surveyed it all surreptitiously in passing, soaking up whatever he could without slackening his pace. As he climbed the stairs, his open palm slid along the banister, caressing it like a blind man, as if to absorb the subliminal information deposited on its surface while he breathed in the stale, Freon-tainted, antiseptic odor peculiar to a well-maintained, air conditioned, but uninhabited house whose windows have remained unopened for too long.

When they reached the second floor landing with yet another flight of stairs to go, the visitor—feigning unsteadiness as an excuse—continued his sensory explorations, laying his hand against the cool irregular plaster of an unadorned expanse of wall, stroking a bit of fluted molding, brushing the edge of a deep-set windowsill with his fingertips, as if testing for dust. Everything visible in the course of this perfunctory, incidental tour revealed a building architecturally at odds with itself. While significant portions of the interior had been made over, simulating the spare, white, uninflected lineaments popularized by contemporary design—the advance guard of a style that would eventually overtake the entire neighborhood—the adjoining areas remained steadfastly committed to their original nineteenth-century features. These contradictory impulses abutted one another, clashing to odd effect and leaving the whole bereft of its identity. What might conceivably have become a triumph of eclecticism resembled instead the product of a doomed genetic engineering experiment, which, in its determination to salvage the best of everything, only created a monstrous amalgam, inevitably marring the virtues of its parts.

At the next landing, his escort pushed ahead, showing the way to Morgan's third floor study—recently appropriated by the Foundation Board as its temporary headquarters—which lay behind one of several identical doors. Grasping the knob, he knocked twice (clearly a signal rather than a request for admission), and without waiting for a reply, opened the door and stood aside, silently inviting the visitor to enter. The room was dimly lit by a chandelier of colored glass grapes and by many small lamps nestled within the bookshelves or placed on the end tables or on the floor, creating little pools of light that only accentuated the depth of the surrounding shadows.

For the present purpose the six-member Board had been whittled down to three—two men and a woman, each of whom had enjoyed a prior association with Dr. Morgan—who had volunteered to serve on the hiring committee. They sat side by side facing the door behind a refectory table at the far end of the room, each with a neat stack of papers and a blank legal pad. Looking up at the new arrival as he entered, they wore the grateful expression of people whose long-awaited moment has finally materialized. They welcomed him, thanked him unconvincingly for coming, introduced themselves in a chorus that drowned out each name in the succeeding one, and invited him to sit down. An oak armchair on his side of the table was the only unoccupied seat available, and he obediently made use of it. A banker's lamp on the table, its green shade tilted in his direction, obscured his view of the committee members and gave the event the atmosphere of an interrogation.

Meanwhile his former escort, Mrs. Morgan's special assistant, had followed him inside and taken up a position behind the triumvirate, leaning back against one of the tall, rain-spattered windows, his arms folded across his chest, reinforcing his resemblance to a bodyguard. His attitude drew the visitor's attention to a seated figure beside him, a figure whose stillness, dark clothing, and imperious posture in an imperious straight-backed chair, he had initially mistaken for yet another inanimate object in the shadowy overfurnished room. Once he noticed this immobile creature of indeterminate age, the visitor may have started to suspect he was in the presence of Dr. Morgan's widow. She was wearing black, although whether this represented an act of mourning or merely a carefully considered fashion choice was impossible to determine, and her hair, pulled severely back from her forehead, mimicked both the sheen and color of patent leather with an effect so uniform that nature could have played no part in its achievement. The somber afternoon cast flickering highlights of agitated raindrops around her head and shoulders as well as those of the man standing by her side. No one introduced her or even acknowledged her presence and the visitor, bowing to protocol, followed their example and averted his eyes, pretending she didn't exist.

Directly across the table from him, seated between the other two committee members, a man who had identified himself as Dr. Morgan's former attorney and chairman of the hiring committee—whose weighty demeanor suggested both the burden and the privilege of leadership—heaved a sigh indicating he was about to speak and, with no further preamble, did so. "To be frank," he said, "your employment history is of grave concern to us." As if convinced this statement constituted a question, he fixed his gaze on the applicant before him and waited, but no reply was forthcoming. The applicant, who had shifted his position to avoid the glare of the lamp and gain a better view of his questioner, was leaning slightly forward with his elbows resting on the arms of his chair. He looked steadily back at the chairman with an attentive, untroubled expression, awaiting further enlightenment. The standoff lasted a few moments before the applicant relented.

"Why?" he asked mildly. "In what sense, exactly."

The chairman amplified. "We have, of course, received some fairly enthusiastic recommendations from a few of your previous employers," he said, wiping his high glistening forehead with a folded handkerchief. "They say you're a quick learner. They commend your diligence, your ready grasp of the fundamentals of what you're engaged in. On the other hand, they do acknowledge finding themselves left in the lurch when you unexpectedly decided you were moving on. We've been obliged to seriously question whether your character suits our requirements. You don't appear to be the sort of person we could rely on to uphold a commitment on any long-term basis. We simply cannot afford to invest in someone who is likely to abandon the position months or even years later, compelling us to begin all over again."

"Ah, yes," replied the applicant. "I see." A muscle in his jaw was working as he mulled over the issue, like someone sampling a challenging foreign delicacy, testing his ability to swallow it without betraying his distaste. "You do understand—don't you—that what you are referring to as 'my employment history' were jobs I took, not a failed attempt to chart a career path. Sometimes a man needs to seize whatever opportunities he can find to keep body and mind together ..." He darted a glance in the direction of the widow but was unable to ascertain whether he had succeeded in catching her eye. "While he's waiting," he added pointedly, with the hint of a conspiratorial smile for her benefit, before turning back to the chairman. "I've never had a mission before. I've never had something I believed I could legitimately devote my life to."

The chairman bristled. "Forgive me, my friend, but this is not about *your* mission. It's about *ours*."

"Precisely. Sure it is. They just might turn out to be one and the same." The applicant risked another smile probably intended to disarm, although it might have struck the chairman as more insolent than genial. At the same moment, coincidentally or not, the widow stirred in her upright chair and rustled. In the absence of a word or any other sign from her, this small, inarticulate movement assumed the power of a commentary, and the chairman, interpreting it as a rebuke, relinquished the questioning with a nod of his head to the woman on his right, who had begun tapping her pencil on the pad in front of her, awaiting her turn.

A former secretary to Dr. Morgan—though not the most recent one—she still clung to a proprietary interest in how his collection, not to mention certain of his possessions and correspondence, were organized and maintained. She still believed she knew where the skeletons were buried and still felt bound to safeguard what she knew, but keeping secrets was not one of her strengths. The strain of residual loyalty, of self-imposed discretion running counter to her expansive nature, had left its mark, overtaxing the muscles around her mouth and marring her otherwise cherubic face. None of the accoutrements of her distant girlhood (the ruby lipstick, the blonde curls, the splashy floral blouse with flounces at the throat and wrists), which she retained in spite of warnings in the mirror, succeeded in softening the severity of the overall effect.

She viewed the new candidate, like all his predecessors, as her potential successor and, in that capacity, as a threat to everything she had jealously protected for so many years—someone bound to critique, revise, undo, and destroy everything she had managed to achieve in the Morgan world. Only a perfect clone could have adhered to her standards. Confronting the man who now faced her across the table, she widened her large blue eyes in a habitual expression of feigned innocence and inquired about his views on the Baconian method of classification and how he thought it related to Dr. Morgan's philosophy. This question was soon followed by a litany of arcane phrases only an archivist like herself with a doctorate in library science would have had any reason to know, and yet seeing him flounder in response reassured her, at least momentarily, that she had discharged her responsibility and exposed his inadequacy to her colleagues.

The third member of the committee, swiping a finger across his tongue for moist traction as he leafed through his sheaf of papers in search of a particular document he deemed relevant, interjected himself into the proceedings. In spite of his embattled role as Dr. Morgan's financial advisor—which had demanded constant and largely futile efforts to restrain his client's profligate impulses—their friendship had flourished in several arenas: as regular opponents on the squash court or across a chessboard, and as intellectual sparring partners, bound by a shared appetite for argument as sport. Perhaps it was in this dispassionately combative spirit that, with scarcely a glance at the candidate, the third committee member pointed out that an essential feature of the job would be introducing Morgan's concepts to a largely ignorant public and wondered what experience, other than that brief stint teaching—what was it, again? teaching foreigners how to speak the English language?—he could claim to have had as an educator. Peering over the top of his rimless glasses and smiling with prosecutorial zeal, spurred on by the silence from across the table, he added: "And after all, could anyone rationally deny the value of experience?"

"If only one knows what to make of it," the candidate murmured cryptically, pressing his palms and fingers together in what might have been mistaken for the gesture of a saint in prayer and plunging that edifice between his knees to keep it out of trouble.

Bolstered by the brief, diffident response to this line of inquiry, the questioner drove his point home by suggesting, somewhat more cynically, that driving a truck or grooming horses or tending bar or clearing away dead trees was hardly appropriate training for such a challenging curatorial position, but when this too failed to get a rise out of the interviewee, he ventured an appeal on economic grounds. In light of the fact that living on the premises as caretaker in residence and unofficial guard was one of the requirements of the job, the Foundation, much as it regretted this necessity, would be obliged to deduct the value of the living quarters it provided from the employee's salary, thereby significantly reducing the anticipated compensation to an amount one would have to admit was scarcely adequate to support a frugal existence.

The candidate looked back at him, squinting against the lamplight. This involuntary narrowing of the eyes intensified a complex pattern of intersecting furrows, like desiccated riverbeds of tears not shed cascading down his cheekbones into the hollows below, mapping the topography of his literate face. "Whatever you consider the job is worth," came his tactical answer, as if he were responding to a riddle or maneuvering inside a fairy tale with a kingdom as the prize.

The former secretary now rejoined the exchange, noting that, upon Morgan's death, significant areas of the collection still remained unexplored and uncategorized, and inquiring as to how the candidate proposed, were he hired, to address such issues given his lack of any relevant background or credentials, whether as curator, educator, archivist, conservator, librarian, restorer, or document analyst.

The ritual of question and answer proceeded in this vein, with the candidate shifting his attention, from one to the other like a spectator at a Ping-Pong match as they took turns lobbing obstacles at him. He sat patiently listening, generally without rebuttal, as they pointed out his shortcomings and his lack of resources to deal with all the pitfalls awaiting him. Paradoxically, the fervor with which the triumvirate marshaled itself against him endowed him with a power he'd never imagined he possessed; seeing them treat him as a threat, he began to realize he might actually be one. Throughout the ordeal, he kept his answers as short as possible to avoid getting into deeper water, and favored the equivocal and provisional over the definitive reply. At last the chairman, convinced that they had succeeded in decimating his chances, inquired perfunctorily, as a prelude to dismissal, "Is there anything else you think we ought to know?" He had not anticipated an affirmative answer, but he got one.

"Surely there are people out there better qualified than I am, at least on paper, people with whom I couldn't hope to compete on that level and wouldn't attempt to try," the candidate began with the deliberation of someone picking out individual words from a poorly organized display. "And please don't confuse this with some flabby attempt at modesty. I'm just stating facts. If we can agree on anything, it's that my many invaluable attributes, whatever they may be," his mouth flickered into a lopsided stillborn smile, "include no university degrees, no certificates of merit, no single-minded training in any of the disciplines you'd find reassuring in a potential employee. But at the risk of sounding presumptuous, I think an iconoclast like Dr. Morgan deserves better, better than some well-trained servant obediently treading in the footprints of established methodology. What I have to offer obviously precludes anything of the kind. I haven't lived a sufficiently cloistered life. I've been busy getting my hands dirty, inviting the world to tempt me with what it has to offer and buffet me about at will. I'm only asking you to consider the possibility that this may be an asset, something you ought to entertain the possibility of embracing. There are worse apprenticeships for a paper conservator than learning how to salvage a dying tree."

As he spoke, one hand had been gliding like a predator along the surface of the table toward the base of the lamp and now, having contacted it, without pausing for a moment or diverting his attention from those he was addressing, his fingertips edged the offending object a few inches further to his left, preventing its light from troubling him any longer. The action—decisive and sly, like the movement of a snake's tongue in slow motion— loosened something in him.

"Look, I understand the gravity of the decision confronting you here. If I were in your position faced by someone like myself, I suspect I'd be equally wary." At this point, the widow—whose natural stoicism coupled with her desire to feign absence while remaining present had so far prevented her from making any discernible movement—suddenly bowed her head. She might have been stifling amusement. She might have merely dozed off. She might have been trying to listen for something only audible in the absence of sight. "Besides," the candidate continued, undeterred by this minor distraction emanating from the dark corner, which he evidently took as a sign of encouragement, "Any one of you, of course, given your experience and the singular advantage of your individual relationship with the man—how I envy you, how I envy you your memories—but all that's beside the point, isn't it? If any one of you were willing and able to serve, I wouldn't be sitting here, would I? So it is not a question any longer of my ability to do a better job than you could, but of the sort of job I might be uniquely able to do if given half a chance." He had attained the crest of his argument. He paused there, contemplating the precipitous descent that lay ahead.

"I may not have known Dr. Morgan, but at least as far as this job is concerned, I have come to know something more important. I have come to know the workings of his mind, maybe as well as anyone alive, if paying scrupulous attention to the evidence counts for anything. It has been the greatest challenge of my life—and its greatest pleasure—to immerse myself in his life's work." The longer he spoke the more pronounced an unidentifiable accent—so imperceptible as to be nonexistent during the first part of the interview—became. It was as if his mastery of English had only been achieved by way of another language, which now, under the pressure of his current excitement and sudden uncharacteristic volubility, returned to haunt his words with an invasion of foreign gutturals, or rolling R's, or suppressed consonants, with Swedish lilts, questioning inflections, the hint of an upper class Briton's lisp (more affectation than impediment), or the extended, multisyllabic vowel of a Southern drawl. To the untrained ear this hodgepodge of accents might have sounded impressive, a sign of a Continental sophistication; to the linguist, it would have suggested a poseur desperate to fit in everywhere, whose attempts to do so only betrayed the depths of his estrangement.

Following a brief account of what he called "the uncanny set of circumstances" that had first brought him into contact with singular philosophy of *Stuff* and of his state of mind several months earlier when he chanced upon the Morgan obituary—all of which induced the three members of his audience to fidget about uneasily in their chairs and exchange anxious, surreptitious glances, fearing this monologue would never end—he continued to make his case: "For many years I have been—and regardless of the outcome of this interview I will continue to be—an avid, devoted, attentive, constantly probing student of everything Dr. Morgan wrote about his intentions and achievements, not just the exquisitely nuanced arguments themselves, you understand, but of the apparent internal contradictions as well, and how even these are part of the ultimate cohesiveness of what he has to say. I've probably read his work more often and more rigorously than the author himself. It's almost metaphysical, the process, as much an act of submission as an act of will, letting the words take hold of your mind the way they do, bending it in their direction. All the same, I have not become so blindly indoctrinated as to have lost my empathy for those encountering his collection for the first time, with no prior knowledge of his work. I vividly remember what it's like to come upon him as an innocent. In many respects, I still am one. I'm still animated by that incurable skepticism which is the mark of the true believer." He paused. "Look, I know I'm not the person you want. But I am here ... Fate or happenstance or luck or whatever you choose to call it brought me. It's just possible I'm what you need."

At the conclusion of this speech, the applicant, slightly flushed, trailed off as disconsolately as an erupting garden hose abruptly deprived of its water supply. He lowered his eyes, convinced he'd gone too far. "Of course, there are no certainties," he said. "In the end, you'll simply have to take a chance on me ... And if not me, on someone else. I may be your best bet."

The chairman seized this long-awaited opportunity to end the proceedings. "I think we have what we need," he said with undisguised haste, turning to each of his fellow committee members for confirmation and making an aborted attempt to rise to his feet as an indication that the meeting was over. It remained unclear as to whether what they needed was the candidate himself or merely the information they'd elicited from him, whether the chairman's statement actually signaled ultimate acceptance or dismissal. The applicant reached down for the satchel at his feet and made as if to leave, but paused in his chair instead, with the satchel perched portentously on his knees, and offered his first wholly unsolicited remark.

"Excuse me for mentioning this, but I thought you ought to know. I've been reading the Collingwood memoir," he said, fingering the satchel's unopened leather flap. "I'm preparing a response. Not necessarily for publication, you understand— purely for my own sake. I just need to do *something*. I don't think

I can endure such allegations and remain completely silent."

These words had a paralyzing effect on the room, as if its occupants regarded motionlessness itself as a defense, as if they believed that remaining very still and ceasing to breathe could magically expunge what had just been said and eliminate the necessity to respond.

Dr. Morgan's scrupulous plans for his posthumous reputation had failed in at least one regard: he had neglected to name an authorized biographer, some distinguished advocate with unimpeachable credentials to tell the story as he wanted it told, thereby cementing, at least for a time, his own version of himself. Presumably, he had been unable to find anyone he considered up to the task. At any rate, given this omission, it was hardly surprising that, absent the inhibiting force of his personality, nothing remained to prevent the jackals from feeding on the spoils.

Within weeks of his obituary—and several months before the publication of *The Man Unmasked,* an exposé by a disgruntled former friend and colleague—rumors began sprouting like weeds in the cracks of Dr. Morgan's once unassailable reputation, rumors kept at bay by the subject's actual existence. Suspicions soon gave way to stentorian whispers that hardened briefly into accepted fact, but then, as rapidly as they had sprung up, promised to evaporate in the face of public apathy about the subject (hardly a household name) and the distractions offered by fresh victims with undefended reputations waiting to be dismantled. *The Man Unmasked* and its attendant publicity breathed new life into them. The book—subtitled *A Reluctant Memoir*—published so soon after Morgan's death, must have been completed years earlier, and had simply been lying in wait to have its say in a timely fashion without fear of retribution, legal or otherwise.

In spite of the author's professed reluctance to expose "the true nature" of the man he claimed to have once "admired above all men," in spite of his regret over what his "allegiance to truth" demanded of him, in spite of his persistent struggle to sound judicious, venom tipped the scales. Epithets ranging from the minor character flaw to the criminal littered the book's pages. The subject was variously depicted as arrogant, vain, cowardly, duplicitous, intellectually dishonest, morally bankrupt, sadistic, and vengeful, each adjective supported by several paragraphs of anecdotes presumably constituting proof. Morgan was accused by the memoir's author—a retired chemist and former colleague, whose standing in the scientific community had mysteriously plummeted in recent years—of plagiarism, theft, fraud, and forgery, impugning not only the validity of his subject's achievements in science but also the provenance and authenticity of many of the most important objects in his collection, as well as the legitimacy of his authorship of *Stuff*, the work that had secured his reputation as an innovative thinker. Nonetheless, Dr. Morgan might eventually have risen above this fairly exhaustive attack were it not for the more pernicious allusion to an incident, or incidents, of pederasty. To those with very long memories and an appetite for chewing on salacious tidbits, the allegations may have sounded vaguely familiar, echoing rumors briefly bandied about in the distant past.

The Man Unmasked resurrected the forgotten question, which, once posed anew, could no longer be confidently answered in the negative. To imagine the possible was instantly to render it probable. The story was at least thirty years old at this point—divorced from its origins, altered, embellished and truncated by time—and of no real consequence to anyone but the participants themselves, both of whom were dead. The aggrieved Collingwood, however, nursing his own sense of betrayal by the man he had once been proud to call his closest friend, managed to parlay it into a parallel narrative of his own victimhood. Was Dr. Morgan, or was he not, guilty of seducing—to use the romantic and possibly euphemistic word rather than the legal term with its violent implications—the adolescent son of his archival assistant one summer when the boy had come to serve an extended internship while his father and only surviving parent was vacationing in Spain. Collingwood dramatized the episode, rendering it more plausible for his readers by introducing vivid, if admittedly hypothetical, details, setting the scene in Morgan's study (the very room in which the applicant's interview was taking place), inventing dialogue for his characters, and providing his own probing insights into the psyches of both victim and perpetrator. In circular fashion, he theorized that if Morgan proved guilty in this instance, the episode could not conceivably have been unique; given the nature of pedophilia, it must in fact have had its antecedents and successors, like so many dependent clauses, each with its own nameless young casualty to be pitied and avenged. Had Morgan managed to muzzle them all with money, Collingwood inquired rhetorically, with promises, with influence, with threats?

Of course, the widow and the Board members had already engaged in lengthy discussions amongst themselves about what they delicately referred to as "the problem" or simply—in an undertone usually reserved for obscenities—"the book," as if to name it would be to further sanction its reality. They had soon agreed that any attempt at refutation would have to be exhaustive, since concentrating only on the most egregious allegations was in danger of confirming, by omission, the veracity of those left unrebutted. A further impediment to action lay in the fear that threatening lawsuits or issuing vociferous denials (no matter how eloquent, no matter how persuasive) would only lead to counterarguments from the other side, thereby keeping the whole question alive before the public in a way that served the author's interests rather than their own. In the end, after consulting legal experts, they unhappily concluded that silence, unsatisfactory though it might be, remained their best available weapon—and neither the title of the book nor the name of its author had since been mentioned in their presence until now. The candidate's pronouncement had abruptly broken the spell.

The chairman, invoking the authority of the widow's presence for the first time with a subtle tilt of his head in her direction, took it upon himself to explain the Foundation's official position to the would-be defender of the faith and to impress upon him how unwelcome they would find his well-intentioned efforts at vindication. The candidate, studying his knees as he listened, was nodding silently. "I understand," he said at last. "Of course it's your decision. I'm sure you know best and, naturally, I have no choice but to respect your wishes." Clutching the satchel to his chest like a symbol of his transgression, he rose from his chair as he had almost done several minutes earlier, but remained standing there before them, evidently at a loss for what his next move might be. "Well," he murmured, in a feeble attempt to mimic protocol and lose himself inside it: "Thank you for taking the time to see me." The familiar refrain led them to thank him in return and to mutter almost in unison their perfunctory goodbyes. And still he lingered. "But is there really nothing to be done? Can any coward with a little time on his hands tear down with impunity a reputation more sterling than his own simply because the one who earned it can no longer defend himself? Christ, isn't death itself insult enough?"

"For all we know it may be only the beginning." These words, uttered in a low voice issuing from the widow's corner—a voice resonant with suppressed irony—were accompanied by a stirring rustling sound betokening movement. With her special assistant at the ready by her elbow overseeing her efforts while scrupulously refraining from providing any unwanted help, the widow got to her feet, slowly, deliberately, like someone monitoring the status of a familiar, recurrent pain, and emerged from the shadows, moving around the table toward the reluctantly departing visitor with both her hands extended. "On behalf of the Doctor and myself," she said—she had always called her husband Doctor, substituting the title like a term of endearment for his given name—"I want you to know how much we appreciate your coming all this way." She took his hand, sandwiching it ever so briefly between both of hers, as if she were surreptitiously passing on a secret note. "We'll be in touch with you quite soon," she said, while her assistant, animated perhaps by some psychic signal, approached the visitor and, in a replay of their initial encounter, maneuvered him toward the door, peremptorily offering to see him out.

When he first accepted the position as the Morgan Foundation's caretaker-in-residence and promised them five years, he may have envisioned it as little more than the latest in a continuing series of respites from his own life. He must have relished the prospect of inhabiting this sanctuary—one he had never even anticipated visiting other than in his imagination— a sanctuary, however temporary, in which to polish someone else's silver, to house rare manuscripts in plastic sleeves, to rehabilitate a broken stool or damaged artifact, to replace labels for displays, to wrest order from disorder, and to share with strangers, to whatever degree his eloquence permitted, his hard-won understanding of the meaning of Dr. Morgan's singular achievement. On several occasions in the course of the ensuing twenty-four years, he had tendered his resignation only to be persuaded to withdraw it each time, inadvertently securing in the process salary increases to which he remained indifferent, and binding himself in exchange to additional ever-lengthening terms of commitment. His departure has been eradicated as an option by his repeated failed attempts to effectuate it. He got the job. Now the job has him. A trap, partially of his own making, is closing round him, holding him fast.

And so today, like yesterday, and like so many other yesterdays that he has lost count and even forgotten when it was he lost it, he once more leads a steadily dwindling little band of visitors up the staircase he first climbed as an innocent applicant for a position that is now the very essence of his identity. He is the caretaker of the Foundation, Dr. Morgan's man, a hired hand of sorts, so safely ensconced within his role that his capacity to excel at anything else has ceased to be a threat. He is here solely to make the dead man come alive. It has become a consuming preoccupation. His work is never done.

In the early days, immediately following the opening of the Foundation to the public as a museum, the caretaker had enjoyed the assistance of a part-time volunteer archivist, as well as a series of summer interns looking to enhance their résumés, who helped him research and catalogue objects in the collection and keep the files in order. Three times a week, a cleaning woman would come with a small crew to erase the signs of trespass, polish that which could be made to shine, and keep the place free of dust. For a brief period, there had also been an annex where the public could purchase miniature replicas of selected objects, as well as assorted novelty items: the red brick building as an eraser, notepaper adorned with the Morgan insignia, or refrigerator magnets picturing an installation wall. Popular as the store and its merchandise had proven to be with shoppers—garnering on occasion more traffic than the museum itself—it nonetheless failed to turn a profit. The Board had long since decided in a vote of five to four that the endowment could not sustain the cost of manufacturing the products, nor the salary of a sales clerk, and had reluctantly shut the annex down.

All those employees had been the caretaker's colleagues. He had monitored their comings and goings, exchanging small talk on a regular basis. Other than a few clerks in the neighborhood hardware stores and groceries, a couple of waitresses and bartenders and regular patrons of a local eatery, and the occasional visit by a friend from overseas who happened to be passing through, they comprised his entire social community. In recent years, though—due in part to financial constraints—he's been largely on his own. The Foundation Board, long since satisfied with the adequacy of its caretaker's performance, had relaxed its supervisory role, confining itself to semiannual assessments of the written progress reports he was required to submit and the occasional unannounced inspection by appointed members assigned to monitor his conduct on the tour.

Whatever passion the Foundation's professed mission had once ignited in its original Board members abated with the passage of time, quenched by the frustrations, both political and practical, inherent in attempting to perpetuate the interests of a dead, and almost forgotten, man. Aside from the widow, all but two of the original six members have either resigned or died. Their replacements—on average about fifteen years younger than their predecessors and twice as ambitious and energetic—had been chosen for their administrative or business skills and were determined to make the entity financially self-sustaining, if not actually profitable, even at the cost of betraying certain principles explicitly stated in the Will. New members had on more than one occasion voted to sell off a few of the collection's most valuable objects to replenish shrinking coffers. They had the advantage of ignorance on their side. None of them had been acquainted with Dr. Morgan, nor had they more than the most superficial knowledge of, or interest in, his work. His name meant little to them beyond its function as the title of a foundation. Inevitably, the reconfigured Board, uninhibited by any residual loyalty to the founder's wishes, began reconfiguring its mandate.

The widow lingered on but her power as a chastening influence had been vanquished by her condition. Suffering from dementia and confined to a nursing home, she spent her days in a reality from which experience of the present and memories of the recent past had been largely obliterated. In their stead, pockmarked visions of her girlhood forced themselves upon

her, peopled by figments of deceased friends and relatives—
her husband included—who taunted her with their ephemeral
presence and ensnared her in old quarrels, many of which had
never actually occurred. For years she had subsisted on memories. They harbored everything she valued most in her adult
life. Now, like a traveler without a passport precluded by a failure to produce it from returning home, she was denied access
to the remnants of her past, now imprisoned somewhere in
an impenetrable corner of her own mind. Every so often, she
would emerge from her blighted state to endure a brief glimpse
of what she'd lost, which only made things worse, leaving her
forlorn, desolate, beached on a strange shore. The disease that
had left her identity in tatters, depriving her of the pleasures
and achievements of her own unique history, offered her in exchange no compensatory eradication of suffering. The dementia was, however, kind enough to spare her any knowledge of
the impending assault on her late husband's legacy, which she
was now helpless to prevent.

Among the many plans of which the widow remained
blessedly unaware was a capital improvement project, currently stalled—but only temporarily—by an ongoing dispute
between the Foundation Board and the Landmarks Commission, a dispute from which the latter was unlikely to emerge
victorious. The Commission—having survived over the years by
contenting itself with a series of pyrrhic victories and by culti-
vating a willingness to compromise virtually indistinguishable
from an appetite for defeat—could not be expected to alter its
long-standing practices by suddenly trying to make a real fight
of it in the Morgan Foundation case.

The Board's proposal, as presently conceived, entailed the
construction of a fifteen-story steel and glass office tower that
would rise imposingly above the site of the Foundation to vie

with its neighbors for its own fragment of sky. Furthermore, in deference to the historic importance of the Morgan Foundation as an antiquated structure (housing what some now believed to be an equally antiquated concept), the original red brick building was to remain intact and functional—at least for the foreseeable future—encased in glass at the base of the modern tower, a mere curiosity as impotent and baffling as a ship in a bottle. The architectural firm hired by the Board to draw up the construction plans and implement the design submitted its self-congratulatory proposal endorsing the proposed edifice as "an homage to the very principles espoused by Dr. Charles Alexander Morgan" and calling it "an exquisite embodiment of the creative tension between—and interdependence of—past and present within a structure that honors them both." This proclamation was perfectly in keeping with the current strategy: to embrace Morgan's little privately funded museum and incorporate it into the new agenda—thereby deflecting any possible charge of breach of trust—and to drag it into the twenty-first century, where it would ultimately wither away on the shoals of its own demonstrable irrelevance.

Given the powerlessness of the widow and the two surviving original Board members—the latter a weary minority resigned to being outvoted in any seriously contentious matter—the caretaker, with his faculties more or less intact and his heart still in the right place, began to see himself, if only by default, as Dr. Morgan's sole defender and last remaining hope for posthumous survival. Although he wielded no political clout, he had inadvertently gained a significant territorial advantage. The Board's absorption in more important matters and its indifference to the museum's fate had effectively ceded to the caretaker sole dominion over the building's day-to-day operations. While he could not have hoped to succeed in his mission by any overt maneuver, his role as an autonomous insider left him free to use his natural subversive ingenuity. During the past year or two, objects had begun to move from one room to another. Others occasionally disappeared from their displays, replaced by something new but almost indistinguishable from the original. No one missed them. No one even noticed. No one was left to care.

On the surface, the caretaker betrays scarcely any awareness of an impending threat. He has cultivated a willful blindness to the ongoing machinations concerning the museum's uncertain future—and, by extension, his own—performing his duties as diligently as if nothing had changed, as if, in the face of his calm persistence, nothing ever would. Had there been a witness to take note of his demeanor when he mounted a step stool in the library, dust cloth in hand, to minister to the books that lined the top shelf, or sat at the workbench in his room copying out the text from one of Morgan's ledgers onto three-by-five cards in his studious penmanship, or set about dismantling an installation untouched for decades, one subject at a time—the green beetles, for example, or the tarnished silver spoons—to make way for a new installation unavailable to visitors until now, his fixed trance-like smile, the tilt of his head, the pursed lips through which a tuneless song escaped might have implied a peculiar serenity, a serenity reserved exclusively for those who, having waged a long futile battle against despair, have finally befriended it and, with a sigh verging on relief, abandoned their last vestiges of hope. The Board could not be blamed for failing to recognize in this dutiful, mild-mannered employee the dangerously single-minded enemy it was harboring unwittingly within the Foundation walls.

This morning when the caretaker arrived to greet his assembled visitors—he counted nine of them, two more than on the previous day—he had forsaken his customary deliberately casual attire (the well-laundered workshirt, fraying a little at the collar, the grey cable-knit sweater with leather patches at the elbows, the pair of ample corduroys cushioning his bony knees), which had almost become a uniform by now. This habitual choice of clothing had long served a dual purpose. From a practical point of view, it protected him from the perpetual chill inside—a carefully monitored archival mandate aiming to prolong the life of the museum's fragile objects—which set the prescribed temperature at sixty-four degrees. Additionally, his slightly shabby informality was meant as a signal to visitors that their guide—unlike the docents and scholars they may have grown accustomed to in visiting most cultural institutions—did not purport to be an expert imparting knowledge to the uninformed strangers temporarily in his care, but rather a uniquely fortunate insider, an impassioned acolyte, willing to share with them something of what he happened to have discovered along the way.

This at least was the first impression he wanted to create, hoping to suggest to his audience, as a kind of corollary, that the building they were now privileged to enter and explore—with its ostensibly indiscriminate curatorial embrace and haphazard installations—would bear no resemblance to the usual stuffy public institution. On the contrary, despite the absence of the original host, it stubbornly remained what it had always been:

a private, if admittedly eccentric, residence permeated by the intimate, unstudied atmosphere characteristic of a place where someone lived, and it deserved to be approached in that spirit, with the instinctive deference of an uninvited guest gaining admittance to a stranger's house when the unsuspecting owner happened to be away.

Such, however, is not precisely the strategic first impression the caretaker is striving for on this occasion. This morning will be different. This morning he has something else in mind. Instead of his regular uniform, he wears today an ill-fitting houndstooth three-piece suit—its padded shoulders extending a couple of inches beyond his own, its sleeves stopping just short of his wrists, its trousers exposing below the cuff of each leg as he walks a glimpse of silky chartreuse sock—which he means to employ as a dramatic feature of the day's tour. Only the shoes, an old pair of thick-soled highly polished brown brogues, can legitimately claim to be his own. The awkwardness with which this borrowed ensemble adapts itself to his body—hanging limp or drooping where it should have effortlessly hugged his frame, stretched tight where it had originally been intended to be generous, and magnifying with each such minor divergence the hopeless disparity between his own physiognomy and that of the man for whom the suit originally had been made—fails to disconcert him in the least. He wears it as impassively as a turtle wears its shell. The visitors, who might otherwise have found the spectacle of their oddly misattired guide unnerving, are evidently blinded to it by the power of his masterful nonchalance. In a triumph of self-effacement verging on a magician's vanishing act, he manages to orchestrate the preliminary transactions and usher his charges into the first room—the room he calls the Overture because Dr. Morgan had called it that—without ever precisely registering on them as a *presence*. He is biding his time, waiting for his moment. He prides himself on being a very patient man.

Once inside, he hangs back, watching over his little group like a conscientious parent presiding over an infant's wobbly first steps as individuals gradually detach themselves from the group and tentatively embark on independent explorations. He makes a study of their rapt or baffled faces, their apathetic frowns, whisperings, the self-protective folding of the arms across the chest, the pensive attitude of fingers poised against a cheek, their sophisticated squinting, the eyeglasses repositioned or removed for better viewing, the frustrated attempts to read the labels, the efforts to get closer, the efforts to remain aloof and keep one's distance. The room, conceived by Dr. Morgan as a Noah's Ark of one-of-a-kind singularities rescued from extinction and butted up against one another with no regard for distinctions based on function, value, purpose, size, material, or source—cries out for explanation and gives none. On the contrary, it acts as a deliberate provocation, designed to thwart the inquiring mind intent on deciphering a pattern.

The caretaker withholds himself. "Don't demand too much," he says in answer to the plea for guidance in the expressions of those who turn at last, somewhat disconsolately, in his direction. "Think *overture*," he reminds them: "It's only an introduction. Be patient. Everything can't be revealed all at once." This is the first lesson in the education—or reeducation—of the viewer who mistrusts his own experience and hungers to be told what he is seeing. As Dr. Morgan intended it should, that education comes in the form of a rebuke that leaves its victim confounded and bereft, thrust back into the isolation of his own restive thoughts. The caretaker has turned this prescribed test into his own benign, private entertainment. He toys with the guests a little. He makes assessments: who among them is ripe for revelation, whose mind is closed, who has concluded the entire enterprise is worthless and is looking for a way out, who prefers to withhold judgment and rely on faith.

Eventually, having decided that the members of his group have endured sufficient torment and are ready for the next adventure, he gathers them again like a shepherd working his sheep, swooping up the stragglers and herding them all toward the narrow staircase leading to the second floor. Each small procession he has conducted through the house has had its own character. Some have been as antic and excitable as the doomed enchanted children of Hamlin pursuing the Pied Piper, some inquisitive but grave, some boisterously irreverent, others merely dutiful, obedient, lackluster. Today's group is distinguished by resignation and a sense of foreboding, as if some inevitable punishment were awaiting.

The tour's route never varies. Twice a day the caretaker must retrace his steps with a new eclectic band of strangers in tow. Whether he takes the lead or—as he has chosen to do on this occasion—assumes a position at the rear, he will be obliged once more to revisit the scene of what he privately refers to, even in the language of his dreams, as the "incident"— a euphemism all the more potent for its imprecision—which permanently scarred the first year of his employment and has continued to haunt him ever since. The site is memorialized by a vacant shiny black plinth, somber as a tombstone, that occupies a darkened corner of the second-floor landing with a label affixed to its front identifying the particulars of that which is no longer there and never will be.

Even now, the caretaker remains incapable of passing the spot without a small, but visible involuntary shudder, to which he has long since grown accustomed but not inured. It is as if each shameful act he had committed in his life—each petty humiliation, indignity, disgrace he'd ever suffered—had chosen this location as its burial plot, which now exuded a collective psychic stench that he alone was privy to. Blood had been spilled here upon the wide plank floor. Stitches had been required. Permanent scars had formed as a reminder.

The culprit was a woman. ("Naturally," is what the caretaker catches himself murmuring sometimes, to his immediate chagrin, when he happens to recall the incident while shuffling through the empty rooms late at night—but he has his prejudices, no point pretending otherwise.) She had been one among a group of possibly six or seven people he was leading through the house on a miserable, snowy afternoon during that first winter when, still very much a novice, he was feeling his way into the new role. His memory of her—for he had practiced remembering, hoping an accumulation of precise detail would help assuage his guilt—was that she had come late, arriving moments after he had locked the door to start the tour. She had been forced to ring the bell to gain admittance, and he, torn between conflicting obligations, had halted the proceedings to answer the summons, and without even considering the alternative, let her in.

Her face was flushed. Her wooly cap sparkled with melting snow. She was already fumbling with the buttons of her coat and apologizing before she was halfway through the door. "You wouldn't believe what it's like out there," she announced triumphantly, implicitly congratulating herself for having come at all. Her excuses consisted of an uninterrupted litany of the tribulations she'd been subjected to by the weather, the traffic, a subway train that pulled away the very moment she reached the platform, all of which had conspired to thwart her best efforts to be on time. She was obviously elated by the experience. A series of exaggerated gestures and facial expressions accompanied her monologue, as if this were a choreographed routine intended above all to entertain. Whether she was habitually tardy by nature, or merely a frequent victim of circumstantial impediments, the situation she now found herself in was obviously not unprecedented. She managed it with the practiced gaiety and confidence of someone who had been obliged to excuse herself many times before and who had been reassured by past experience that she would inevitably, without much effort on her part, achieve forgiveness.

At last, having successfully exonerated herself, at least to her own satisfaction, she finished extricating her body from the complex wrappings of her coat and—refusing to entrust it to the unattended rack in the vestibule (a temporary substitute for the as yet unrealized convenience of an official checkroom)—draped the garment over her arm, gathered up the rest of her belongings, completed the obligatory transactions, and joined the other members of the tour who had been left waiting with undisguised impatience near the museum entrance. In the twenty-three years since, the caretaker's memory of the incident had somehow attached itself inseparably to the woman's dark, voluminous coat, the exact nature of which had, with the passage of time, undergone several subtle mental transformations. The mohair fabric of his original early recollection currently exists in his mind, after several intermediate metamorphoses, as some kind of glossy imitation fur.

Once the tour commenced, the woman continued, deliberately or not, to draw attention to herself. "How absolutely fascinating," she would proclaim periodically, as if the phrase amounted to a considered opinion. Every now and then, someone who happened to be standing nearby would be enlisted in support: "Perfectly marvelous, wouldn't you agree?" she'd say, turning to the closest stranger. Or, "Have you ever seen anything like it in your life?" The caretaker conducted the visitors from one room to the next and up the staircase to the second floor, pausing here and there along the way to point out objects of special interest or to introduce an underlying principle of the collection that may not have been self-evident to the uninitiated. His style at the time was diffident rather than effusive, subject to hesitations, even the occasional stutter. From time to time, in the course of a brief monologue on the theory behind a certain installation, one that relied heavily on quotations memorized from *Stuff*, he would lose his train of thought midsentence and be forced to change the subject to save face.

The little group climbed the stairs in his wake and assembled on the landing in front of the black plinth and its offering: a glittering pale green leafy cabbage-like affair some five inches in diameter, standing unprotected upon the smooth rectangular surface. Instinctively, everyone kept their distance, intimidated by the intricate formation and obvious fragility of the object before them, apparently as hard and translucent as glass and as prone to shatter. From where each had chosen to stand, the label on the front of the plinth, with its careful, tight handwritten lettering, proved all but impossible to read. The caretaker was obliged to intercede on behalf of his visitors, from memory. He knew the legend well.

In spite of its symmetry and ornamental appearance, the object was believed to have been created without any human intervention solely by an act of Nature. "Or, if you prefer, given the celestial element involved," the caretaker added soberly, with no trace of irony, "an act of God." According to the generally accepted theory of its origin, it had been forged some fifteen million years ago in Bohemia, a remote region of Czechoslovakia, by the impact of a meteorite colliding with the surface of the Earth. While experts had identified other examples of the same species, none had come to light to rival this particular specimen: its impressive size, lightness, and clarity, and its singular absence of any of the visible flaws—occlusions, cracks, chips, pitting, intermittent streaks of opacity, or broken fragments—characteristic of all the rest. Dr. Morgan had acquired his specimen in the late 1960s from an amateur geologist of his acquaintance in payment of an old debt and—due to its age, rarity, unusual chemical composition, and multifaceted hard translucent beauty—had assigned it a place of honor in his collection. Since that moment it had occupied its distinguished position at the head of the stairs, confronting everyone who arrived at the second-floor landing with the imponderable fact of its existence.

Following his rendition of the object's provenance and history and its role in Dr. Morgan's philosophy of the museum, the caretaker permitted his audience a few moments to gape and murmur in contemplation of it before urging them to follow him down the narrow hall to the next display. With the superficial docility of children on a school outing, they formed themselves into a line, leaving the late arrival trailing along in last place. They never reached their intended destination. Almost at once, a sound, abrupt and jagged as lightning, stopped them, signaling catastrophe. They froze like strobe-lit figures caught in mid-motion, listening while a cascade of minor repercussions spawned by the initial crash grew progressively fainter and gradually died away. This all took a matter of seconds. In the subsequent hush, each member of the group, as if stung by the irrational suspicion of his own guilt, seemed bent on simulating innocence. No one wanted to look. "What happened?" a solitary voice asked plaintively.

The caretaker turned and began making his way back along the phalanx of visitors to investigate, edging by them one by one as they moved aside, pressing themselves up against the wall to let him pass, brought suddenly back to life by his action. "Stay where you are, all of you," he said. "Please. Nobody move."

The woman at the end of the line held her position a fraction longer than the others, blocking his path and obscuring for a moment his view of the plinth standing empty a yard or two behind her. She faced him, pale and wide-eyed, her mouth slightly ajar, looking simultaneously bewildered and defiant. As he attempted to get past her, his glance—at least from her perspective—amounted to a wordless accusation. "I didn't do anything," she protested. "I was nowhere near it." Her face had assumed the injured expression of a victim unjustly singled out for blame when an entire community, an entire social order, perhaps the intractable nature of humanity itself was actually at fault. Although her proximity to the scene of the accident and the fact that the coat she had been carrying over her arm now lay draped around her shoulders might have aroused suspicion, there had been no witnesses. It had all happened while everyone's back was turned. Who could be certain that the artifact, having exhausted its preordained finite time on earth, had not suffered some sort of internal chemical breakdown and spontaneously exploded from within—its destruction as inexplicable as its creation.

The caretaker stopped to survey the aftermath, stretching wide his arms to keep his visitors at bay—the curious, the impatient, and the indifferent alike, now temporarily his prisoners looking to escape—while he contemplated the spectacle that lay before him and made an assessment of how to cope. The sound alone had so vividly evoked catastrophe that the actual scene, appalling as it was, looked almost anticlimactic compared with the devastation he had already envisioned a moment earlier. Dr. Morgan's precious artifact had been reduced—or multiplied, or at any rate, transformed—into innumerable fragments, some the size of a peach pit or the butt end of a pencil, others only visible as tiny glints of light. They carpeted the bare wooden floor surrounding the plinth and lay scattered haphazardly over the descending stairs.

Maintaining a safe distance from the outskirts of the disaster to avoid doing any further damage by a careless movement or misstep and using his body to block the people now clustering at his back, he took a deep breath, undid the buttons of his woolen shirt and took it off to serve as an impromptu receptacle for whatever he might succeed in retrieving. Leaving the scene unguarded, abandoning it to the whims of these indifferent strangers for any reason—whether to go in search of a flash-light or a vacuum or a more appropriate vessel for the salvaged particles—would clearly have been the height of folly. Instead, obliged to use his ingenuity and make do with what he had, he stripped down to the pale indecency of a thermal undershirt with its patches of discoloration at the armpits and a few old food stains that no amount of vigorous washing had managed to eradicate—a state of undress so much more unseemly in this company than if he had actually been naked to the waist—and squatted down, spreading the discarded shirt upon the floor by his side and smoothing out the creases. He could feel the assembled audience watching. He could feel them studying the exposed tuft of hair at the nape of his neck or counting the bony ridges of his spine pressed against the fabric of his undershirt.

His hands became his broom and dustpan. In wide sweeping gestures, they set about skimming lightly over the uneven surface of the floor, gathering together the shattered fragments and scooping them up to deposit into his waiting sacrificial shirt. Given the inadequacy of the lighting, a great deal depended on feel alone; anything sharp he encountered, whether he could see it or not, was presumed to be something he needed to re-trieve. In the process, stray bits of each handful's contents that he attempted to relinquish would remain behind, clinging stub-bornly to his damp palms where they glimmered like distant lighthouses in the whorls and creases (the same creases that en-couraged certain women he once knew to insist that they could read his fate). When he tried to brush the remnants free by rubbing his hands together, he had to use the utmost delicacy: exerting a fraction too much pressure wound up embedding invisible crystal splinters into his skin, which would eventually have to be plucked out one by one.

As he worked, clearing a path through the wreckage just wide enough to allow his trapped visitors to exit single file without doing any further damage, he kept inching his way forward toward the staircase, gradually reaching deeper into the thick of what lay strewn before him. "I'm very sorry," he said, addressing them at last, but without permitting himself a glance in their direction or the slightest pause in his progress. "This is going to take a few minutes. I'm afraid you're all going to have to wait." His announcement was met with disgruntled protest from various quarters. Several people reminded him they had responsibilities of their own, prior engagements that could not be postponed, pressing needs beckoning to them from the outside world, lives that required living. They'd had enough of Dr. Morgan's museum for one day.

The mounting pressure at his back, both psychological and physical, threatened to become an avalanche, making his task increasingly urgent. Getting rid of them was now his sole objective. For the sake of efficiency, he temporarily abandoned the salvage aspect of his mission—resolving to return to it as soon as he was alone and could attend to it in peace—and concentrated his efforts exclusively on creating a safe passage for the group. He had almost reached the staircase—having successfully carved out a narrow immaculate valley of dark wooden floor that stretched out invitingly behind him between mounds of glittering debris swept off to either side—when he caught sight of a pale green stalagmite about the size of his thumb nestled among some smaller shards that lay just beyond reach, near the base of the empty plinth. It looked to be the jagged broken tip of one of the artifact's outer cabbage leaves, the largest, the most intact—and therefore by far the most desirable—fragment he had yet encountered. Postponing its rescue for even a moment would have been intolerable.

Still crouched on his haunches, still wary of accidentally

crushing something salvageable underfoot, he swiveled around a few degrees to face his prize, and, extending his long limber torso to its full length, stretched out his right arm to retrieve it. He almost had the thing—it lay waiting directly beneath his hand—when an uncharacteristic moment of carelessness, probably brought on (as he suspected later) by a premature savoring of his triumph, cost him his balance and his instinctive attempt to break the fall impaled his palm onto the gleaming upturned spike with the full weight of his body behind it. The shock tightened his grip.

Judging by his subsequent recollection—which was soon all he had to go by—the initial sensation had nothing to do with pain. He had known pain before; like anybody his age, he had experienced it to varying degrees on multiple prior occasions. This was something altogether different. This had as little in common with pain as with pleasure. The flesh, as if anticipating the intrusion, had offered no resistance. It parted willingly, embracing the invading foreign object like a preordained wound welcoming the weapon it had been destined for. The jagged point entered the center of his palm at the intersection of two deep creases, which those women from his past, the heavy-lidded would-be oracles brimming with ominous interpretations, would have called the head and fate lines. It penetrated his entire hand, its tip emerging on the dorsal side between the tendons of the middle and index fingers where the veins made arcane crisscross patterns of their own that looked like writing.

After a momentary pause, blood began to flow and once started was disinclined to cease. With its lethal treasure still intact, the caretaker gingerly cradled the injured extremity against his body as if it were a trapped bird he had foolishly volunteered to nurse, and got to his feet. A stain was seeping into the fabric of his undershirt, turning it a peculiarly vibrant shade of red and making it look as if he'd been stabbed in the belly. He stared down at himself, mesmerized by the enigma.

His visitors seized the opportunity to take charge. The emergency must have invigorated them. Heedless of the broken stuff beneath their feet, they pressed in around him, full of unwanted offers of assistance, creating a general hubbub of suggestions and advice: ordering one another to call 911, to fetch a towel, to get the victim to a seat, to help him down the stairs. Although the reluctant beneficiary of their attentions kept shaking his head and saying no, insisting he was okay, really, and perfectly capable of managing on his own, they ignored his protests. Someone got hold of him by the elbow and refused to set him free.

As to whatever may have happened after that, he could no longer be certain, having since confused memory with hallucination and fantasy with fact, each—at least in retrospect—as plausible as the other. Had the guilty woman, his eternal nemesis, really offered him her white linen handkerchief to stop the bleeding or was that ironic detail purely his invention? Had he really grabbed her by the shoulder from behind with his one good hand while she was preceding him down the stairs and demanded she submit to an immediate examination of her coat on which he thought he had detected tiny remnants of Dr. Morgan's artifact about to be smuggled off the premises?—although, in all fairness, he had to admit that whatever he'd seen glittering there also bore a striking resemblance to scattered droplets of melted snow.

He wasn't sure how he wound up at the hospital, whether one of the departing visitors had forcibly accompanied him or whether he had somehow made it there on his own. He thought he remembered waiting his turn in the company of fellow sufferers in a remorselessly well-lit room with plastic chairs and a green-flecked linoleum floor, where competing injuries and ailments acted as status symbols; where the overdoses, the moaning, the gunshot and stab wounds, the bleeding, the maimed, the semiconscious vied with one another for the best, most urgent claim to attention in the pecking order. He thought he remembered watching someone write *deep puncture wound* on his emergency admission form, as if it had become his new identity.

What he knew for sure was that his right hand and the precious fragment embedded in it—which by that time he had come to regard as a single inseparable entity—were eventually subjected to some artful form of surgical intervention that succeeded, without too much additional damage, in detaching them from one another. What he knew for sure was that he had received six stitches in his palm and two on the back of his hand. What he knew for sure was that his attempt to reclaim the thing that had caused his injury—"the dangerous piece of broken glass" as they called it—was passed off by hospital personnel as an eccentric whim until his outburst over the matter reached such a pitch that they resolved to indulge him, retrieving it from the trash so as to finally be rid of him.

It must have been later that afternoon, or possibly the next, that he had resumed his salvage activities at the museum, eventually recovering two hundred and forty-seven individual pieces of the shattered artifact—yes, he counted them, every fragment, every shard. The exactness of the tally comforted him, solidifying his grasp on the event. The broken bits, shrouded in a blue sheet, were tucked away where guilty secrets like to hide, at the back of a closet shelf. Keeping them was a way of clinging to the hope of resurrection, the possibility that he just might, in some inconceivable future, manage to put things right again.

His subsequent session before the Board probably went as well as could have been expected. Thanks once more to the widow, his perplexingly loyal advocate, and her subtle powers of persuasion, the members did not vote to fire him. They did not demand he make reparations or renounce a portion of his salary in compensation for the lost object—an amount especially difficult to estimate at this point since the thing had instantly increased in value merely by ceasing to exist. In their collective wisdom, they may have calculated no censure at all was the most effective punishment they could inflict on him. He stood before them, his bandaged hand an emblem of disgrace, and claimed full responsibility for the "incident," citing a shameful lack of vigilance on his part coupled with a desire to enhance the visitors' unfettered experience of the place that had undeniably put the safety of its treasures at risk.

Because he doubted they would find it credible, the caretaker did not share with them the real source of his anguish, but he remained haunted by the fact that he had always quietly disapproved of the now demolished artifact. He'd considered it aesthetically pretentious—like something one might discover in a bourgeois china cabinet—and altogether too flawless to be worthy of its place of honor in Dr. Morgan's singular collection of the strange, the marvelous, and the astoundingly mundane. Although he recognized the somewhat absurd egotism inherent in his guilty conscience, he nonetheless remained convinced that his underlying contempt for the object—his failure, literally, to care for it—had been the actual cause of its destruction.

The incident marked his loss of innocence and the museum's loss of innocence as well. In spite of his pleas and promises, new rules were promptly enacted. Stricter policies were put in place. Less and less was left to chance or to the appointed guardian's autonomous supervision. The building Dr. Morgan had envisioned as a sanctuary of exploration and independent discovery for every visitor, professional and amateur alike, was suddenly besieged by cunning security devices signaling distrust. Leashes threaded through the spines held books in place. Shatterproof glass shielded objects from the onlookers. Alarm systems, rigged by unseen wires, waited to emit their hysterical screech the moment anything happened to be jostled out of place. Barriers were erected to keep people at a distance. Posted signs cropped up, issuing warnings (*Do Not Touch, No Food or Beverages Allowed, Private No Admittance, Personal Belongings Must Be Checked*) that conjured transgressive notions which might otherwise have never come to mind.

This period—which in the end turned out to have been mercifully brief—came to be referred to by the caretaker in his private lexicon as the Reign of Terror. Not that he could really blame the Board for its actions. Its primary responsibilities concerned the material, rather than the spiritual, maintenance of the place: there was valuable property on the premises in need of its protection. He, on the other hand, in trying to be true to Dr. Morgan's principles, had ironically become implicated in the betrayal of them. Whatever moral authority he might have accrued with the Board as a champion of Morgan's cause had been tainted by his role in the incident that had precipitated the new restrictive measures, crippling his ability to argue against them.

Nonetheless, in spite of his failure to make his case, within a year or so the original status quo had largely re-established itself, not as a result of his subtle acts of vandalism (although the caretaker had selectively given that a try, unfastening a few leashes, disabling alarms, hiding posted signs by rearranging a display), not as a result of any official decision to relax the rules, but thanks to the healing powers of attrition, neglect, and amnesia. With the passage of time, devices failed, memories faded. The old ways seeped back into the void. And yet, even today, more than two decades later, telltale signs still linger, scars remain.

A persistent numbness still afflicts the core of his right hand where a raised welt of pale flesh, vaguely sickening when touched, has concealed or destroyed—some might say, permanently altered—the pattern of his fate. All the same, that lack of feeling in his palm fails to prevent a heightened sensitivity to cold, or a dull throbbing sensation that comes and goes from time to time with no apparent cause.

Instead of the posted notices, most of which have been removed, there is the caretaker's low voice judiciously reminding people of the rules when necessary—telling them to keep their distance, that touching is forbidden—with an apologetic inflection suggesting his unspoken disapproval of the policy. In the absence of real barriers, there are still symbolic ones. Ghosts of suspicion tarnish the atmosphere. And there is still, of course, half-hidden in its darkened corner, the ominous presence of the empty plinth around which this morning's group of nine visitors—unlike most of their predecessors—have instinctively gathered, studying what isn't there as earnestly as the fabled crowd admired the magnificence of their naked emperor's new clothes, compliantly refusing to accept the evidence of their own eyes.

The caretaker waits on the landing behind them. The Dürer portrait, filched from its original place in the Overture, hangs on an isolated bit of wall adjacent to the plinth, watchful as always. In a gesture of overt familiarity that helps bolster his courage, the caretaker hooks a thumb onto the watch pocket of his unfamiliar vest and leans back against the newel post as they attempt to satisfy their frustrated curiosities on their own. "As you have no doubt observed," he begins in a leisurely congenial drawl, "something is missing." The sentence captures his audience's attention and relieves them of the need to probe further. They give themselves over gratefully to what he has to tell. Like a verbal magician, he conjures the missing object for them out of words, not as it actually was, but as he believed it ought to have been: something rough, irregular and ominous, embodying the violent clash of elements out of which it was created. He sees his vision mirrored in their rapt expressions and concludes he has done well.

"It used to be the introductory note of Dr. Morgan's symphonic installation on the nature of glass," he continues, spurred on by the success of his opening gambit, "but thanks to a wanton act of carelessness, the exhibit has been closed for some time now. It soon became apparent that without its pièce de résistance the display of glass specimens had lost its meaning and ceased to add up to a coherent study. And herein lies the Achilles heel of Dr. Morgan's curatorial genius. The very subtlety and brilliance of his meticulously orchestrated ongoing conversation among objects often makes the loss of any single element enough to destroy the eloquence of the whole."

In answer to the inevitable question from a visitor as to the fate of the missing artifact, he offers a version of the incident leading to its demise that deviates in so many particulars from what actually occurred as to be labeled, at least by some humorless straight talkers, a lie—although in the caretaker's mind he may merely be embroidering on the truth for the pleasure and edification of those he is in the process of deceiving. "Well, the world is a fragile place. Full of fragile things," he muses in conclusion, as though providing a fable its required moral. "It needs looking after."

In light of this knowledge, the visitors might have been inclined to linger, but the caretaker doesn't give them the opportunity. "We'd best be getting on. There's lots to see," he says, gesturing toward a half-open door and, following his lead, they begin to negotiate the cramped labyrinthine displays of the second floor. They weave their way from room to room, filing past glass cases, peering into the dim recesses of cabinets, opening shallow drawers by invitation, and under their guide's watchful eye, poring over the minutiae on display inside. His low soothing voice—offering them hints, pointing out obscure connections—casts its spell.

In accordance with Dr. Morgan's object lesson in typology, topics introduced in the Overture by means of a single isolated example are revisited in these rooms in depth by myriad kindred ones: given the infinite variety of leaves, what is the fundamental nature of the thing we know as leaf? This vexing question, which goes to the heart of Morgan's thesis, turns out to hinge as much on issues of language as on biology, science, or philosophy. Definitions expand and contract in response to shifting needs for inclusion or exclusion. After some time spent dazzling, deluding and enlightening themselves, the visitors emerge from the last of the contiguous series of rooms, their minds reeling with questions of likeness and difference, to find themselves at the opposite end of the landing in front of a staircase leading to the next floor, access to which is thwarted by a braided rope bearing a homemade sign that spells out in block letters: PRIVATE.

The caretaker ceremoniously undoes one end of the rope and lets it fall, savoring the effect of this unexpected tacit invitation on his little group. Hesitantly, one by one, the nine of them, propelled on by their host's ambiguous evaporating smile, head up the stairs toward their next destination, forming a tight cluster of indecision on the landing. They make for a timid bunch. Their excitement at the prospect of a spectacle implicitly denied to others is tempered by uncertainty: the privilege they have been granted may be one they would prefer to have renounced, but there is no turning back. The triumph of Morgan's complex installations lies behind them. His widow's triumph lies ahead.

Here on the top floor lie the residential quarters of the house. This is where the private Dr. Morgan, driven to retreat before the growing demands for space and time of his perpetually expanding collection—"the insatiable beast," his wife had called it, to which the more he gave, the more it seemed to need of him—had taken refuge. These are the rooms in which, for most of his last decade while in pursuit of the demands of his great passion, he had lived and worked and slept and sometimes entertained, pretending to the best of his ability to go about the rituals of daily life in the manner of an ordinary man. This is where, since his death, in fulfillment of a promise made only to herself, his widow had staked out the territory for an installation of her own, preserving as sacred even the most mundane artifacts of her late husband's existence. Some of his devoted admirers regarded her project as a deliberate parody of Dr. Morgan's stunning achievement, the revenge of a jealous spouse on the rival that had stolen from her the affection she deserved. Others saw it as a bereaved woman's tragic, ill-conceived expression of idolatry.

In either case, regardless of her motives, the widow turned out to have been right. "The public craves the personal touch," she had said years before, addressing the Board in its early days in defense of her proposal. "Much as we all appreciate the ambition and complexity of the Doctor's great undertaking, we must admit it's all a little arcane for the ordinary person. What most people really want is some access to the private man. They want to find out how he lived and see the commonplace things he chose to surround himself with. They want to be able to poke about among his personal belongings for the reassurance that, no matter how brilliant or famous or rich or aloof he may have been, he was basically just another human being, not unlike themselves. True or not, why deny them what they want?"

The effect of these upper rooms on their new selectively chosen audience confirm the widow's point. As the morning's nine visitors move about Dr. Morgan's study (painstakingly, though perhaps a bit too creatively, restored in accordance with the widow's mandate to the condition in which her husband had left it the day he departed on his final fatal journey), the look of strained puzzlement begins to seep from their faces. Unlike their recent experience on the floors below, where every marvel they encountered represented one more challenge in a vast imponderable mystery begging to be deciphered, the scene before them now is full of familiar stuff, evocative as a stage set, and requires no interpretation. Here in this comfortable, well-appointed, unremarkable room, where the sobriety of dark wood and heavy woven fabrics is punctuated by the occasional paragon of modern furniture design, by plastic souvenirs, diplomas and awards, and a cacophony of idiosyncratic mementoes, the imposing figment of the absent Dr. Morgan, stripped of the armor of his curatorial intent, loses much of its impermeable luster, leaving the great man's artifacts exposed to the hazards of prying eyes and the casual inspection of paying customers.

The tall casement windows, facing south and blinded for the moment by the refracted glare of the noonday sun, throw a pattern like prison bars across the disorderly array of papers on the desk and superimpose it upon the ornate flourishes of the faded Oriental rug. The stereo is on and the muted voice of an aging tenor issues from the speakers, risking everything in traversing octaves and challenging rapid-fire lyrics with the abandon of an aerialist. Books line the walls—three thousand four hundred and twenty-two in all, the caretaker announces, giving his audience the benefit of his fetishistic absorption with numbers. The impressive total, as he goes on to point out, includes not only the volumes in plain view crowding the open shelves from floor to ceiling, not only those resting facedown on the arm of a chair or lying open on a book stand or a hassock waiting for their pages to be thumbed, but the forty-two leather bound ledgers segregated behind leaded glass doors in a locked cabinet all their own, each with a year emblazoned on its spine, which account for all the known volumes of Dr. Morgan's journals. Only the last one, dated 1988, the year of the author's death—which would have contained no more than eleven entries at the most and may in fact never have existed at all—remains missing. To this day, the well-advertised standing offer of a substantial cash reward, supplemented by a diligent professional investigation conducted both at home and abroad, has evidently failed to unearth the coveted item.

The visitors let loose in the room have been exploring its contents on their own with the tentative, suppressed excitement of liberated sheep, but their investigations begin to embolden them. A few brave souls succumb to the temptation to touch things, surreptitiously stroking the back of a chair or running a finger along the spines of books as if it helped to make the titles legible, astonished that, unlike what they had been led to expect downstairs, the transgression when observed provokes no rebuke. The tenor's solo, still barely audible beneath the murmured commentaries circulating through the room, devolves into a duet—a lovers' quarrel actually—in which the two singers, locked in a barbed exchange, continually contradict, outdo, and eclipse one another in an impassioned battle for the last and longest-lasting note.

After offering brief replies to a few questions from his more inquisitive visitors, the caretaker retires to a corner to watch over the members of his little group—fragmented now into random couplings, a threesome, a pair of solitary stragglers—as they probe about among the objects of their respective curiosities. They peer at the photographs, some in silver frames stationed on the shelves like impromptu bookends or crowded together on an end table in the manner of those accumulated family portraits that decorate a piano, boasting of happiness. The image of Dr. Morgan is everywhere, like a stocky cutout figure deftly inserted into one scene after another, apparently unaffected by his surroundings or by the passage of time. His unmistakable large head with its proud unruly hair makes his companions—the balding contemporaries and doomed starlets, the politicians, celebrated writers, musicians and other over-achievers of his era posing beside him with feigned gaiety or gravity—look as insignificant as props.

In spite of—or because of—efforts to the contrary, Dr. Morgan's absence permeates the room. It emanates from the orphaned chairs with their plump, uninflected seat cushions and empty arms, from the immaculate, dustless surfaces, the unlit lamps, unopened windows, unread books, from the signs of order or disorder. Even the cultivated tokens of ordinary life are of no avail: the pair of well-worn velvet slippers positioned neatly by the hearth waiting in vain to welcome a familiar pair of tired feet; the uncapped fountain pen, abandoned by its writer, lying useless on a sheaf of papers while its ink dries up; the reading glasses languishing beside an open dictionary; the half-smoked, recently extinguished Cuban cigar, its tip apparently still moist, resting in an ashtray, as if poised there hoping to be reclaimed.

These hapless clues bristle with false promises. Isn't it conceivable, they keep hinting in a sly whisper, that the former resident, now dead for more than a quarter century, might still be inhabiting his study as a persistent ghost and, having only just been unexpectedly called away, could return at any moment to retrieve his cigar and catch these trespassers in the act of violating his private sanctuary. Of course, the nine trespassers in question happen to be rational, sophisticated people for the most part, unlikely to be troubled by such subtle intimations of the supernatural. The vicissitudes of daily life have sharpened their need to detect the trick lurking behind every miracle. Skepticism is their god. And yet the past couple of hours lingering under the spell of Dr. Morgan's museum, with its insistent demands on the imagination, has apparently undermined their usual capacity to dismiss without question the existence of certain unseen things and left them abnormally vulnerable to the pleasures and terrors of illusion. All sorts of dubious possibilities begin to infiltrate the tidy certainties embedded in their minds.

Their absorption in the things laid out before them—things redolent of secrets long withheld, of buried answers to unasked questions—prevents them from registering, beyond a subtle sympathetic vibration in the chest, the tremulous orchestral flourish that finally overwhelms the contentious duet playing itself out at subdued volume on the stereo, or from noticing how the orchestra, once it has achieved this end, continues to hover with monotonous uncertainty on the brink of an unfulfilled crescendo.

What does succeed in distracting them from their investigations is the sudden, unexpected stirring of the caretaker in his forgotten corner. As if propelled forward by the portentous musical cue subliminally accentuating the drama of the moment—or by some other force disconnected from his will—he abandons his refuge and approaches the center of the room, moving stiffly, laboriously, like someone wading out into the sea against a strong opposing current. On reaching his destination, he assumes the awkward pose of a mannequin. All natural physical grace has sacrificed itself to the burden of his strange attire, and his body, no longer entirely his own, is now voluntarily enslaved to its clothing in a complex symbiosis that obscures which entity—the body or the clothes—may actually be responsible for animating the other, which is lending the other life.

He stands there, feet firmly planted, confronting the newly reassembled audience whose attention he has now succeeded in capturing, and begins slowly rotating his torso from right to left on the axis of his hips, providing each onlooker a brief, but optimal view of the virtues of his borrowed ensemble. These include the subtleties of its wool and cashmere blend, its expert seaming, genuine horn buttons, and the shocking contrast of its chartreuse silk lining, a hidden asset, waiting for a convivial moment to reveal itself whenever the jacket got removed. The formal, studied manner of his presentation suggests months of preparation leading up to the event, months of planning, choreography, and solitary rehearsals in the mirror to determine how the thing might best be done. At last, with a grandiloquent gesture in the direction of his own person, he begins to speak.

"What you have before you here is an original, custom-made, double-breasted, three-piece suit belonging to—" he places an open palm reverently against his chest in the vicinity of the wide, old-fashioned lapels "—to Dr. Charles Alexander Morgan, one of twenty-four produced for him on order by his personal London tailor. The other twenty-three, as you will soon be able to see for yourselves, are still hanging safely in his bedroom closet. This particular one, however, far from being selected at random, has a unique—one might even say, tragic—history."

He extends an arm in the direction of the onlookers, an arm

so rigid in its woolen casing that it does not appear to belong to him at all, having more in common with a prosthesis than the actual limb of a living creature. His hand is cocked at the wrist, fingers splayed, briefly exposing for those in his audience curious enough to look, the little mound of tortured flesh at the center of his palm, the souvenir of his old disgrace. "Here, touch it, if you like," he says, offering the foreshortened sleeve for their inspection. "Come on. Please. I need you to make it real for yourselves." But the move only causes those nearest him to flinch and draw back involuntarily, as if they'd mistaken the invitation for a threat. Nonetheless, their reaction fails to staunch the flow of his prepared discourse.

"This is the suit Dr. Morgan chose to wear on that cool overcast fatal Monday, the 11th of January, in the city of Karachi in 1988, when he ventured out from his hotel into a busy street on the way to what notations in his pocket calendar—this calendar," he announces, lowering his voice for emphasis, as he withdraws a slim brown leather notebook from an inside breast pocket and thumbs through the contents for their benefit—an action that manages to reveal almost nothing in the process and proves merely tantalizing, since most of its pages are blank—before secreting it back in place and resuming his account. "An entry on the critical date in question, January the 11th, indicates he must have been headed for a three o'clock appointment with a local dealer in antiquities and archeological contraband, a scheduled appointment which, as fate would have it, he could not keep. What you are now looking at, ladies and gentlemen, is the last suit Dr. Morgan ever wore. The suit he died in."

The caretaker takes a deep breath that might easily be mistaken for a sigh and surveys the nine stupefied faces of his spectators. Five mouths are agape. Twelve out of eighteen disbelieving eyes are staring back at him—or at the suit, he can't be certain.

One woman's long manicured fingers are pressed against her lips, stifling whatever is threatening to emerge. A bearded man is glowering. "What sort of sick game is this?" someone asks. A girl bows her tawny head in a futile attempt to become invisible while, a few feet to her left, a couple exchanges conspiratorial glances and begins inching backwards toward the door, contemplating escape. "Not yet," the caretaker says quietly, stopping them in mid-flight with nothing but the chastening power of his voice. "There are things you need to know." Some sort of trial seems to be in progress that everyone now present will be required to endure.

Apparently persuaded by the reactions of his audience that his initial sally has achieved its aim, the caretaker ventures further. Bending over his right leg, he points out a dark stain on the fabric between shin and thigh where the threads have given way, leaving a tear just large enough to provide—when the knee is flexed, as his is now—a glimpse of the flesh beneath. "This is where the full weight of his body first made contact with the grimy pavement when he fell. And here, too, at the shoulder— see? The dirt of the Karachi street still remains embedded in the cloth, along with what is probably a little Dr. Morgan blood."

An isolated passing cloud has suddenly extinguished the sunlight from the room and the captive witnesses, their vision momentarily baffled by the change, can barely distinguish what they actually see from what they are being invited to imagine. The caretaker's mellifluous, hypnotic voice flows on unabated. "History owes a great debt to the anonymous hospital worker who, sometime after four forty-seven p.m. local time, when Dr. Morgan was officially pronounced dead—although the medical records confirm that he had long since surrendered consciousness and irretrievably ceased to be himself, ceased to be anyone, for that matter—gathered up the patient's personal effects and, being either too principled or too cowardly to succumb to the temptation to pocket a few valuables on the chance no one would miss them, inventoried the whole lot."

He enumerates the contents for them in a kind of chant: "The Cartier watch, still keeping perfect time; the double-buckled Lobb shoes, an English size 10, specially made to order to accommodate each unique bunion, protrusion, or misshapen toe; the monogrammed blue silk Charvet shirt and matching tie; the linen handkerchief probably used earlier in the day to wipe a brow or daub away the dampness from an upper lip; the engraved fountain pen that went everywhere with him, even though it had been known to leak from time to time and stain the inside jacket pocket it was kept in—Look!" Once again, with a triumphant gesture, he shows off the chartreuse lining, this time pointing out a small inky blemish resembling a squashed bug.

He proceeds with his inventory. He tells them about the passport, less than three months short of its expiration date at the moment of its sudden obsolescence, the pages covered in official stamps documenting a decade's worth of international travel in pursuit of the next elusive treasure. He describes the standard issue color portrait of the bearer, the way the formidable head challenges the edges of the picture frame and how the studiously solemn expression, presumably defying the photographer's ritual insistence on a smile, is permanently pockmarked and distorted by the imposition of the embossed seal of the United States.

The litany goes on. No item escapes mention. "The marcasite cufflinks (Dr. Morgan's own design, of course); the alligator belt; a wallet housing a disorganized accumulation of bills in multiple currencies, along with two travelers' checks, a single credit card, and a couple of receipts stuffed in at random; a plastic pocket comb with two four-inch silvery hairs still tangled in its teeth; a folding map of the city bearing three *x*'s marked in pen to indicate, we must presume, intended destinations; the tortoiseshell eyeglasses he must have been wearing when he fell because one lens is cracked and the left earpiece bent hopelessly out of shape ..." The caretaker is savoring each word as if it were the incarnation of the object itself that he was in the process of caressing. "Nine loose coins amounting to thirty-nine rupees; a matchbook from a local dive with some figures scribbled on the inside flap; a pair of silk socks, these socks, the socks I'm wearing now ..." Pinching a bit of trouser leg between thumb and forefinger with a kind of professional delicacy, he thrusts a toe toward the leery onlookers as evidence while he continues his remorselessly exhaustive list. "A silver case for business cards, a leather one belonging to the damaged eyeglasses; the appointment calendar I showed you; some bits of pocket lint (as proof of thoroughness, I suppose); a sticky crumpled paper candy wrapper; a ribbed cotton undershirt—you know, the sleeveless kind; blue boxer shorts, size medium according to the label; a toothpick, a used one, I suspect; and a single piece of jewelry, the thin gold Tiffany wedding band, painstakingly swiveled off the swollen lifeless finger of his left hand by that conscientious hospital employee whose name we'll never know." While he spoke, his hands had involuntarily been mimicking the action he was describing, but now that he is done, they fall helplessly to his sides, useless appendages bereft of any function.

The caretaker blinks several times in rapid succession. "All this stuff," he murmurs. He wears the dazed expression of someone startled out of a dream into an unfamiliar reality, trying to clear his vision in order to ascertain where he is and who he is supposed to be. He looks in the direction of his audience, as if for answers, but they give little back. Since he began his recitation some moments earlier, the surroundings have changed.

The stereo has gone quiet except for a low, all but inaudible hum, signaling persistent plaintive readiness. The errant cloud has finally torn itself to shreds and is drifting off, relinquishing its hold on the sun and leaving it behind, depleted by the encounter. The room feels suddenly wan and colorless, like a casualty of too much washing.

The nine people stand before him, penitents held captive not by the usual methods—locked doors, or chains, or prison bars, or brandished weapons—but by the seductive power of their host's voice, and by their own ambivalence, which keeps vacillating between fascination and revulsion at the unfolding spectacle. Once a group of disparate individuals separated by conflicting impulses, they have formed the instinctive, unspoken alliance of strangers confronted by a common threat. They are breathing in almost perfect unison. A suspicion has been growing in their midst, spreading its contagion from one to the next until it envelops them all. What if the mild-mannered guide they have been following through the house for the past hour or two, whose instructions they have meekly been obeying, and upon whose knowledge and wisdom they have relied, should in fact turn out to be one of those tragic madmen one encounters in lurid news reports who, after years spent nursing unimaginable psychic wounds in silence and successfully masquerading as an ordinary, harmless person, suddenly turns on his neighbors, his co-workers, a schoolyard full of children, and—provoked by nothing more than a wrong word or look— annihilates as many of them as possible before doing away with himself, taking his secrets with him and leaving the rest of us, with the help of volunteer psychiatrists and sociologists, to theorize about his motives and worry over what could have driven him to it; the sort of person, in short, whose whims it would be prudent for strangers to indulge.

"I suppose you could mistake all this for mere ghoulishness," the caretaker volunteers in response to his audience's palpable discomfort in his presence. "But there's a point behind it all, I promise. It goes to the very essence of what Dr. Morgan was aiming at, the reason he created this place and devoted himself to it. How can I make you see?" A note of desperation infects his voice. For the first time that day, he glimpses the possibility that his carefully rehearsed strategy may fail to win converts. This loss of conviction on the part of their putative leader proves even more disconcerting to his visitors than the bravura performance they have just endured. Uncertainty repels them like a bad smell. Their eyes begin darting everywhere, alive with exit strategies.

He might have wanted to tell them more. He might have wanted them to know in detail his version of how all the stuff had eventually made its way back home, neatly wrapped in plain brown paper tied with string, like packaged discards from the friendly local butcher; how, in the manner of a chaperone, the brown parcel of personal effects accompanied the temporary coffin housing the owner's corpse, two mismatched traveling companions sharing space aboard a cargo plane on the journey back to where they'd started from together a mere two weeks before. He might have wanted to lead them deeper into the recesses of the upstairs sanctuary, into the waiting bedroom and adjoining bath, both so carefully prepared to reveal what they'd been hiding all these years. But having saved the best for last, the reluctance of these chosen people—chosen by chance, perhaps, by some mere accident of timing, but chosen all the same—to accept what he is offering, their apparent inability to recognize how deeply they themselves are implicated in it all, dissuades him from proceeding in the direction he had planned.

"You will soon forget me," he says instead. "And I you. Just as those you love, on whose devotion you so fervently depend and who profess themselves incapable of going on without you will soon begin forgetting, too. Or, worse still, will misremember, only to lose you in a miasma of reverence or remorse. What else can you expect of memory, that flabby capricious muscle, so prone to distractions, self-justification, embellishment, delusion."

A fidgety little man at the rear of the group can restrain himself no longer. "I think I've had enough of this. I'm out of here," he announces in a startlingly high-pitched voice, cinching up the belt of his safari jacket as a demonstration of resolve and taking a few bold steps towards the door. The words are intended to stimulate action, not just his own, but that of his fellows; a few people go so far as to glance in his direction, but no one makes a move to follow. Paralysis prevails. It's as if the time they have spent in this place surrounded by Dr. Morgan's things in the company of Dr. Morgan's man has gradually instilled in them a state of passivity they are now incapable of throwing off, as if there were something in the vaguely fetid air hostile to free will, depriving them of any desire for independent action.

In the absence of confederates, the would-be defector's courage fails him, leaving him painfully conscious of his sudden self-imposed isolation from the pack, equally incapable of rejoining the others or of following through on his threatened departure. He lingers disconsolately on the island of carpet beneath his feet, stranded midway between his former comrades and his anticipated freedom, an outcast on the fringe of a lost opportunity.

The caretaker takes up the challenge anyway. "Go on, go then if you must," he says, addressing the entire group with a dismissive wave of the hand, as if he were in the act of making them disappear. "Or stay if you prefer. It hardly matters in the end. Even as you stand there, smugly swaddled in your swaddlings, propping up your fictional personas with freshly blackened hair or reddened lips or whatever transparent masquerade helps you pass for who you think you were or hoped to be, oblivion waits, smiling. Whatever made you think you could escape? Sooner or later we all wind up a pile of empty clothes and worthless keepsakes and sad, abandoned furniture, one last revenge on former friends and relatives now burdened with mounds of stuff to defile, destroy, or auction off. That's the ultimate legacy: whatever's left behind of you in everything you happen to have touched along the way, everything on which you've inadvertently leached away bits of yourself in passing—those flecks of dead skin, the stray hairs, the oily fingerprints, the sweat, the drool, the dried up blood and other fluids. That's what you'll inevitably become and what you will, with any luck, remain, thanks to the impressionable objects you've come into contact with—stone and wood and cloth and metal—things with no agenda, no cause to plead, no interest in you other than to do what they can't help but do: to simply hold you and to keep you and preserve you in all the ferocious tenderness of their sublime indifference."

He speaks with the impassioned equanimity of someone who has nothing left to lose, or more precisely, someone for whom any loss would be counted a kind of victory. He can harbor no illusions about the impending repercussions. Exposure is inevitable. He has finally gone too far. Complaints against him will be lodged with the authorities. His words will be misquoted, his transgressions reported on and perniciously embellished. Once more, he will be summoned before the Board like a delinquent schoolboy and called upon to defend his actions. Reprimands will have to be endured, some suitable form of punishment meted out. Even banishment, the ultimate threat, may be in the offing. All this no doubt he can foresee, but he no longer has the power to silence himself. Besides, it's probably too late for silence now. He presses on.

"Don't you even *begin* to get it yet? This is what lies at the root of the Doctor's reverence for the object: the unique unadulterated particles of history embedded in each one of them from the humblest paper clip or paper coffee cup to the rarest irreplaceable treasure. History's last hope rests here, in these mute, unborn, undead enemies of time. Without them and the place to keep and care for them as they deserve, we'd all wind up orphans of some interminable present with no past solid enough to cling to, no illusion of a future up ahead." His left eye has begun to twitch and while he speaks he rubs at it impatiently like a cranky child awakened from a sweaty summer nap.

"Where else do you think history resides? Do you really think it's about something as ephemeral as words? Do you actually believe the stories they've filled our heads with, those lies and mangled truths concocted in a futile effort to impose a reassuring pattern on the random by assembling disparate events into some arbitrary chronological chain of cause and consequence. Wake up, for god's sake! Look around you. Are you blind? Don't you see what the man has done here? Don't you feel the power radiating from the things inside this place—yes, partly on account of the simple fact that, despite their encroaching obsolescence, they threaten to endure and outlast all of us, these seething carcasses of what once was and is no longer—but also because of the terrible pull they exert on one another. Don't you feel it? Don't you feel how desperately the hammer craves the nail, how ardently the etching congeals itself around the contours of its frame, a magnetism so intense you could easily wind up an unintended casualty of the undertow."

He manifests the peculiar fluency of someone who has honed his conversational skills without the benefit of anyone to talk to, substituting for the more ordinary forms of verbal intercourse extensive monologues conducted solely with himself, unimpeded by interruptions or contradictory opinions or even so much as the implicit rebuttal on the face of a skeptical listener; someone in the habit of embracing with equal fervor any side of a complex, vexing question as a kind of exercise to keep the mind alert and test its intellectual flexibility, pitting one adopted viewpoint against another in a contest which—given the perfect parity of the participants—can only achieve victory by arriving at a stalemate.

"Look," he continues, "no one disputes the fact that every single object on display is first of all defiantly a thing unto itself, a gloriously purposeless, self-sufficient thing with all its own idiosyncratic physical attributes. But on the other hand, consider this: in the absence of a lock—or the concept of a lock—what is a solitary key but a sort of cripple, a strange lost incomprehensible entity yearning for a reason to exist? What can they possibly make of such a baffling artifact a thousand years from now when keys and locks have long since grown extinct? Relationships change everything. Below us in the rooms downstairs—could you have really failed to notice?—even though nothing moves and nothing speaks, a veritable riot is going on. The place is teeming with petty quarrels and competitions, with forbidden assignations, conspiracies, alliances, unlikely kinships, and attractions and repulsions. Didn't you catch the uncut diamond in its case winking impudently at the shiny lump of coal across the way? Or the virgin candle, conceived to be devoured slowly by a flame, inclining helplessly in the direction of the nearby unlit match, its doom and destiny? Weren't you even the slightest bit intrigued by the hourglass, the sundial, the cuckoo clock, and the rest of their kind clustered together in a corner of the second floor carrying on their interminable debate over the nature of time and how to measure it? The strategic distance between any one thing and the next—or the way they're poised in apposition or collusion—

transforms them all. Isn't this how society itself purports to function? For better or worse, each member is made smaller, larger, darker, lighter, rounder, flatter, richer, poorer, stronger, weaker, plainer, queerer in contrast to whatever winds up in its vicinity. As, for that matter …" He hesitates a moment on the brink of an unexpected twist in his disquisition before delivering his conclusion, "As are you, my friends."

The caretaker scrutinizes the small amorphous blob of humanity in front of him, which keeps shifting, contracting, reformulating itself in the manner of a single living organism. Its eight component parts, as if dissatisfied with the degree of their proximity, have been steadily closing ranks, seeking warmth or comfort or a semblance of safety, while the solitary ninth member lingers in their wake, like a drop of spume cast off by the undulating sea. At this point, the entity can shrink no further without risking inadvertent physical contact with itself. Even now, breaths commingle. A shoulder is in danger of brushing up against a powdered cheek; a finger must contort itself to avoid an unprovoked encounter with a stranger's thigh.

From the standpoint of invidious comparisons, the nine people do not fare terribly well in the eyes of their host. One man's distinctive nose becomes an unfortunate parody of all other noses. The sumptuousness of a woman's dark complexion turns everyone else ghostly. Each individual set of characteristics serves as a tacit rebuke to the very nature of someone else's, making oddities of them all. The entire spectacle strikes the caretaker as simultaneously comic and pathetic, sending him into a fit of soundless laughter, which leaves him momentarily helpless, nearly doubled over at the waist, his torso trembling in an effort to suppress the outburst. "Sorry," he gasps, when at last he manages to regain his composure. "But really, you know, you'd best beware your neighbors."

The man with the beard, who has been following the circum-
locutions of the caretaker's thesis from the start, frowning all
the while under the awning of his dark brows, finally settles on
what he evidently regards as a satisfying retort, one that only
hints at his considerable erudition. "This is sophomoric anthro-
pomorphism gone mad," he fumes, obviously spoiling for an
argument, much to the dismay of his companions who begin to
fear this new engagement of the enemy will, at the very least,
prolong indefinitely what has already proven to be a seemingly
interminable stay in purgatory—prolong it, or possibly result in
something even worse.

"Be that as it may—but why so bloody supercilious?" the
caretaker responds, embracing the indictment with an eagerness that suggests it may be precisely the sort of reaction he had
been seeking all along: to flush out at least one person in this
eerily compliant crowd who would care enough to risk fighting
back. "I'm pretty sure Dr. Morgan and I are not the only ones
susceptible to the irrational adulation of inanimate objects,"
he continues. "Just take a look around. What about the young
woman on your right, for instance—the one who cannot bear
to face me for some reason, can you, darling?—fiddling end-
lessly with those silver bangles on her wrist in the grip of some
remorseless private catechism."

The target of this observation is unable to resist the challenge. Without altering the downward angle of her head or ut-
tering a single word, she raises her eyelids ever so slowly, as if
she were painstakingly adjusting a pair of window sashes, and
fixes the caretaker with a look she has no doubt perfected in the
course of navigating the shoals of her relatively brief existence,
a look designed to make adversaries of either sex wilt in shame
or pity, or even possibly in fear. Confronted by those disconcertingly pale eyes of the luminous peeled grape variety in all

their steady defiant vulnerability, the caretaker—like most of the young woman's prior opponents—turns out to be the one who blinks first, rapidly turning his attention elsewhere.

Choosing as his next victims the man and woman who had earlier in the day—it feels now so very long ago—failed in their half-hearted surreptitious attempt to flee the place unnoticed, he persists, elaborating on his initial response. "Or the couple over there behind you," he says, "flaunting their identical silk scarves like the flags of some rogue nation to remind us—or to remind themselves, perhaps?—that they belong together." He singles out the man with a knowing conspiratorial look suggestive of some unspecified exclusively male bond, which succeeds in isolating him from the woman by his side and makes him the sole focus of the question. "And although they may appear to be two people," he adds, "they are probably at this point barely even one—right?"

The female half of the alleged unit flushes under the sting of this gratuitous attack. An uncommonly tall person like her companion, she has been genetically condemned to spend the better part of her life looking down on most of those around her, and this perspective on the world, so easily mistaken for innate superiority, has wound up embedded in her psyche. The shock of finding herself dismissed as an object of derision by a patently inferior being—and a half-demented one at that—leaves her nearly gagging on outrage and, as a consequence, abnormally inarticulate. "This is the most unspeakable—what kind of a ..." she begins in a cross between a whimper and a growl that falls woefully short of its attempt to sound defiant. "You really are beyond belief," she manages at last before turning to her partner in an unspoken plea for rescue, to which his response proves a disappointment: in light of his failure to hazard a suitably scathing verbal riposte, the act of placing a chivalrous arm around her shoulders proves a peculiarly impotent gesture.

The other occupants of the room, their curiosity sufficiently aroused, are now scrutinizing the couple to assess for themselves the accuracy of the caretaker's remarks. A casual glance is enough to confirm for them the superfluousness of matching scarves. Gender differences aside, the two people resemble one another in so many salient particulars—in stature, coloring, a certain coarseness of the features, even the trendy, erratic ministrations of the barber—that no one could be blamed for a momentary confusion as to which of them was which. They appear to have succumbed to the powerful attraction that felled Narcissus, drawn inexorably to the familiar upon recognizing it embodied in the other. A more scrupulous examination would of course eventually uncover the inevitable dissonances—in the shape of the eyes, for instance, or the earlobes, or in the individual character of their gestures—but these differences only serve to highlight the fundamental similarities they share.

Although no particular animosity had existed until now between the unfortunate couple and their fellow visitors—nor any real basis for animosity aside from the instinctive suspicion attendant on most encounters between strangers—the present situation, simply by pitting the seven detached observers against the helplessness of the observed, creates in and of itself an implicitly hostile confrontation. To make matters worse, without specifically intending to do so, the observers—in their eagerness to disassociate themselves from the two victims and to remain more or less invisible in the hope of escaping the sort of abrasive scrutiny the couple has just endured—wind up implicated as passive allies of the persecution. The mere act of looking—exacerbated by the refusal to submit to protocol after a decent interval and look away—becomes as bruising as an actual physical assault.

The objects of this unwanted attention hold their ground, but not without betraying, by a stiffening of the posture and of the muscles around the jaw, a suppressed inclination to do otherwise. The man tightens his protective grip around the woman's shoulders. "What the hell do you think you're all gaping at!" he demands in a belated attempt to make amends to his companion for his previous reticence. She joins in. "What's wrong with all of you? Has everyone gone nuts? Why are we letting this—this contemptible—this pathetic creature do this to us?" These essentially rhetorical questions go unanswered and the caretaker, having succeeded in stirring things up a bit, has lost interest and moved on, returning to his original interlocutor, the imperious man with the beard who might be presumed to have started it all and who must not be permitted to escape unscathed.

"And what about you, yourself, sir?" he inquires mildly. "Hiding there behind your carefully cultivated underbrush, stroking it for reassurance every now and then so you can keep pretending it successfully conceals the sneering mouth or weakness of the chin or whichever shameful defect you fear might give your game away. Whereas all it really does is show us there's something you need covered up." In the wake of the arid silence greeting this remark, he casts an appraising eye over his remaining prospects, contemplating the possibilities like a hungry carnivore savoring the unsuspecting creature that will soon be his next meal. No one is safe now. Each is destined for his own dreaded moment in the sun.

"Go on, clutch that monogrammed alligator handbag with its treasure trove of dirty little secrets to your breast for comfort," he says with renewed vigor, zeroing in on the woman with the long purple fingernails before tackling her nearest neighbor, the fashionably undernourished creature to her left who gazes back at him, presumably—or so he fancies—from behind a pair of impenetrable red-framed owlish sunglasses: "Is this pure style, or do you really fancy you've successfully deceived us about where you're looking and exactly what you're looking at?" Deliberately, one by one, he dispatches the rest: the failed escapee in the safari jacket and scuffed up cowboy boots ("I guess it's worth the inconvenience of pinched toes to gain yourself the illusion of a couple of extra inches") who still hovers near but not quite at the door; an earnest, well-scrubbed woman with a single braid ("that greying, shrinking remnant of your good old Hippie days") beaming vaguely in his direction with the immaculate certainty of the true believer; and, finally, a scrupulously bald, ruddy-cheeked young fellow in a business suit sporting a golden stud in his right ear ("to proclaim your status as a renegade, perhaps, and absolve you of the need to act the part"). His words, aimed each time at some sacred personal talisman, draw everyone else's attention to it and, in doing so, annihilate its power with the ruthlessness of a blowtorch, leaving each of his reluctant guests unprotected and, one by one, bereft of cover. Their fragile alliance, unable to survive the onslaught, now lies in tatters, and they shrink from one another, shriveled, shamed, stripped of their illusions as irrevocably as the inhabitants of Eden after that fatal taste of the forbidden fruit.

These acts of verbal devastation are followed by what might briefly pass for an apology of sorts: "But who am I, you might well ask," he volunteers ruefully. "Who am I to begrudge you your material comforts, regardless of the form they take? Or your deceits for that matter, your harmless petty affectations. We're all entitled to whatever we can get away with, whatever we choose to cling to or hide behind or caress while we face the terrors of the everyday before the ax falls, which—in case you have momentarily forgotten—it inevitably will, whether it's decades from now, or years, or months, or—who knows? —it could be only minutes. There's really no excuse for some rude upstart like me to come along and rumble your disguises as if they were no more impenetrable than flimsy bits of gauze a blind man could see through. Doesn't a civilized society rest on the presumption that each of us will quietly pretend to buy whatever it is the rest of us are selling, that so long as I agree not to notice what you're up to, you'll probably do the same for me? Well, the covenant is broken now. Of course you take it personally. It *is* personal. For some of us, it's about as personal as it gets."

He has the flushed, sweaty look of someone suffering from the heat, although given the actual temperature inside—even up here in what they call the "living quarters," where objects and their needs still take precedence over humans—that heat must be internal, something exclusively his own, self-generating, like a fever. Everyone else in the room remains, if anything, a little cold.

"Look," he says with a solicitous expression calculated—though not entirely successfully—to reassure. "I mean no harm. I don't know any of you well enough for that. But neither am I about to let you get out of here scot-free." He allows the implicit threat to dangle a moment while he attends to the distraction of his borrowed clothes, which have turned adversarial, adhering to his person in undesirable ways, stunting his every move, thwarting his ability to breathe. Ridding himself of some of these impediments takes temporary precedence over his main objective. He cranes his neck from side to side, trying to relax the shirt collar's stranglehold, which—although originally made to accommodate a much thicker neck than the one now protruding from it—has somehow contrived to shrink for the express purpose of tightening itself, as if in protest, around the interloper's unfamiliar throat. When the fingers of both hands attempt to come to his rescue, they prove incapable of collaborating and keep working at cross-purposes, fumbling uselessly at the collar button as if the task demanded of them required skills far beyond their level of expertise. Rather than coaxing the recalcitrant button free of its restraining buttonhole as intended, his impatient fingers wind up detaching it from the shirt entirely. He stares in bemusement at the small forlorn object in his palm, a torn wisp of thread still clinging to it like the tail of a lost spermatozoa, and, after a hasty unsatisfactory survey of the room, deposits it for safekeeping in an empty silver ashtray on the desk. Dr. Morgan's suit jacket is next. The caretaker seizes it by the lapels and struggles his way free, inadvertently pulling the sleeves inside out. The violence of his movements has caused a bit of shirt tail to come untucked, which now droops unnoticed between vest and belt as morosely as a dead dog's tongue. Leaving the garish lining exposed, he folds the jacket with exquisite care and lays it over the back of the nearest armchair, smoothing out the wrinkles.

His preoccupation with these distractions has broken the spell. The people in the room trade furtive, inquiring glances, probing for consensus. By turning away, however briefly, from his captive audience, by abandoning his post as the persistent fulcrum of their attention, the caretaker has relinquished his dominion and left behind a vacuum, which—despite his visitors' hesitations, their perplexing ambivalence at the possibility of liberation, despite their atrophying capacity to initiate an action—sucks them in, burdening them with an opportunity they had been desperately seeking but now no longer appear eager to seize. All the same, there is a noticeable, if reluctant, drift toward the exit.

The caretaker collapses into the waiting armchair, slumping into its depths with a great show of lassitude, and observes the receding human tide as it gradually begins to desert him. Some are sidling away as they say crabs do, others inch backwards. No one has the courage to simply turn and leave. "Abandoning me already?" he asks from his cushioned refuge, then adds, almost as an afterthought, "Well, in that case, you'll probably be needing these." He withdraws from his trouser pocket a set of about a dozen keys of disparate styles and sizes, which dangle from a ring hooked on his index finger. They produce intermittent notes of dull metallic music, clinking against one another as he keeps them swinging slowly to and fro in a deliberately tantalizing fashion, like someone toying with a mesmerized kitten.

The departing visitors, looking as bewildered as sleepwalkers trapped in a collective dream, pause in their retreat and take a few moments to digest the implications of this unanticipated obstacle looming between them and the outside world. It is the man with the beard who finally takes command on their behalf, striding forward in his self-appointed leadership role to within a foot of the caretaker's slouching seated figure and extending his upturned palm in a peremptory fashion. "Hand them over. Now," he says, hoarse with suppressed indignation. The caretaker only smiles and slips the bunch of keys back inside his pocket, safely out of reach. "I don't intend to deny myself the pleasure of escorting you out the way any decent host would," he says, getting slowly, laboriously to his feet. Recent events have apparently sapped much of his strength. The two men stand there face to face, both breathing heavily, though for different reasons, so close to one another now that neither can make a move without retreating. The caretaker still wears his fixed, insolent smile, which—as the moments pass and the smile refuses to fade or change—ceases to be a human expression at all, but rather some hideous caricature of one, like the mocking grimace of a carnival mask, a look his opponent can only regard as deliberate provocation.

They have arrived at an impasse, one that threatens to last forever, since both grow increasingly incapable of backing down the longer they refuse to do so. Only the unlikely intervention of the woman with the alligator bag manages to save them—not to mention the other occupants of the room—from what promises to be an endless state of suspension. Abandoning the seven paralyzed companions with whom she has been lingering in the neighborhood of the study door, she approaches the bearded man, her progress a little unsteady thanks to the delicate high heeled summer sandals she had unwisely chosen for the day's outing, and lays her free hand in a strangely intimate, placating way on his forearm, gently tightening her grip, her long purple fingernails sinister as talons on his sleeve. She murmurs but a single word. "Don't," she says. This peculiar monosyllabic appeal to reason—or is it rather an appeal to gallantry?—nonetheless prevails upon him. He wilts under its pressure. The stubborn, outthrust chin sinks toward the chest, the shoulders sag and, with a single backward step, he yields the caretaker free passage.

There follows almost immediately an unruly headlong progress down three flights of stairs, the caretaker in the lead, while the others—no longer allies in a common cause—jostle recklessly for position in his wake, as if salvation might well depend upon securing an advantageous place in line, regardless of whatever misfortune might befall one's neighbors in the process. The building, unaccustomed to such abuse, trembles at the clattering of eighteen hard-soled shoes upon its unprotected stairs, which groan in protest, and at the brutishness of all these unfamiliar bodies barging through the stillness.

The impatient visitors soon find themselves back in the long, narrow first floor gallery where their journey into the labyrinth of Dr. Morgan's psyche had begun. From this reverse perspective, the room—although identical in all its particulars—now manifests itself as a mysteriously altered version of the one they had originally entered, resembling it only insofar as the dim, distorted, two-dimensional image in the mirror resembles the reality it allegedly reflects, or as much as the home of one's childhood, however meticulously preserved, can be said to resemble the house one revisits on a nostalgic pilgrimage years later as a middle-aged adult. All the proportions have shifted; the relationships have changed. Nothing is different and yet nothing is the same.

The curatorial decisions governing the organization of the room, which had at first struck the newcomers as so deliberately random and chaotic, suddenly look serenely inexorable, one thing impinging on the next as the inevitable rationale for the existence of its neighbors. Orphaned objects assembled here like so much scrap are orphans no longer. A child's worn left shoe bereft of laces, a coil of hemp, a jewel-encrusted Russian Easter egg poised on end, a tarnished ladle with holes punched through its bowl in a star-shaped pattern (presumably to drain off liquid), a glass eye staring helplessly, relentlessly at nothing, an Indian arrowhead, a small framed pen and ink rendering of a dense forest choked with underbrush, the skeleton of an umbrella, a telephone receiver trailing its crimped cord, the displaced Roman nose of a lost marble statue, a fossilized crustacean, a stethoscope, a paper clip, a tortured tree branch, petrified and turned to stone—all members of some complex extended family with their own indispensable roles to play—commune with another across a wasteland of irrelevance, each an answer to the others' prayers.

Not that any of the departing visitors, in their eagerness to escape the building and regain the world they used to know, are paying much attention to their surroundings, nor—even if they happen to glance around in passing as they hasten by the central vitrine in pursuit of the receding figure of their soon to be ex-host—can they begin to account for the transformation in the nature of what they see. Still, it remains too palpable to be ignored. Nothing looks superfluous anymore, or inessential. It is as if, in that recent interval while the people were elsewhere and otherwise preoccupied and the room had been left deserted, an invisible network of intersecting pathways, like a map of veins and arteries, had sprung up in their absence, tracing the hidden connections among all things. The obvious mundane proposition that whatever change had taken place in here must logically have befallen the observers, rather than the observed, is instantly dismissed in favor of some act of magic, or metaphysics.

At the far end of the room, where the sliding mahogany doors remain pulled shut, creating the brief illusion of a faded negative image in which darkness is beckoning at the end of a dim tunnel, the caretaker stands guard blocking the exit once again and warning of "one last piece of business to attend to." Based on past experience, his followers might have expected something like this and, lacking the will to join forces in a physical assault upon their jailer, find themselves at this point too weary to protest. Instead, letting the frenzy for immediate liberation drain out of them, they emit a collective groan, which is enough to pass for what is known as patience.

The caretaker centers himself on the vertical crack where the two doors meet and leans back against the glowering mahogany. A narrow, misdirected shaft of light, originally intended to dramatize the contents of a shadow box, slashes across his left cheek and lights up a corner of his eye. He raises a hand to his brow in a wilted salute to protect himself from the glare as he begins to speak.

"I cannot in good conscience allow you to cheapen this experience by simply releasing you as if you were no better than a bunch of listless sightseers on some interminable world tour, dragged against your will from one legendary monument to the next, wondering all the while when you'd be allowed to stop marveling and go home, back to the impregnable oblivion you came from where nothing will intrude to remind you that you ever left. No," he says in answer to an unasked question. "No, there must be consequences." He scans their wan, averted faces, looking from one to the next, but they all avoid his gaze, as if that could deflect whatever new blow to the spirit he is about to inflict upon them. "That's what scars are for," he adds. "And amputations. They prevent you from denying the fact that something really happened, something that cannot be undone."

An involuntary groan escapes the little man in the safari jacket who is leaning his elbows on the edge of a vitrine as if, in the absence of its support, he would be incapable of remaining on his feet. "Can't you just get on with it," he whines under his breath. "I'd like to get out of here sometime before I die." Everyone is struggling to endure. Even the woman with the braid, retreating still further behind the curtain of her vacuous smile, has lost a good deal of her impermeable serenity. The caretaker shifts his weight from one foot to the other, which liberates him from the intrusive spotlight, leaving it to spill across the dark wood behind his shoulder like a delinquent splash of paint.

"Freedom will come soon enough," he says reassuringly. "But freedom—like anything worth having—comes at a price. Haven't religions been telling us for centuries—perhaps out of genuine conviction, perhaps just as a marketing ploy— that whatever enlightenment we may hope to attain depends upon our willingness to make the necessary sacrifice? Well, you're going to be allowed to leave this place, but in order to get out of here you're going to have to leave something behind. Call it an exit tax. Getting out should be at least as expensive as getting in, don't you think? So come on, who'll go first? Make me an offer."

95

In the absence of volunteers, he proffers some suggestions of his own: he would, for instance, be willing to take the alligator handbag and its contents off its lovely owner's hands, or relieve the couple of their matching scarves, or liberate the perpetually smiling woman from her tyrannical braid, the thing—he ventures to say—that has held her captive for so many years, as if she, rather than her hair, were the appendage. A pair of custom cowboy boots might do, he adds, as would a false front tooth, a wedding ring or some other well-worn amulet, a hat that has been serving as a comforting disguise, perhaps some spectacles, possibly even a faded snapshot of the wife and kids. "But choose carefully," he warns. "It must be something precious you can hardly live without if it's going to mean anything at all. Giving it up has got to hurt a little—like ripping off a flap of skin. One day it could turn out to be enshrined as all that's left of you. Make it count."

The tall woman with the spiky hair has already taken hold of one end of her scarf and ever so slowly, inexorably, almost in the manner of a striptease, is sliding it off from around her neck. Her companion stands beside her with his head tilted toward the ceiling, arms folded securely against his chest, and gazes down upon the state of things along the arc of his formidable nose. Observing the woman's movements and recognizing what she is about to do, he reaches out to restrain her, but she escapes his attempt at intervention with a shudder and darts him a quick accusatory glance, as if he were to blame for everything. "No, I don't want it anymore. It's ruined. He's ruined it," she says.

She steps forward and delivers her limp offering to the waiting caretaker, lays it somberly across his outstretched palms like a bereaved mother surrendering the lifeless body of an infant, and retreats back to her place among the others, who are beginning to weigh the implications of this capitulation on their own actions. Her partner, faced with what he can only regard as a pointed personal rebuke, evidently concludes he has no choice but to follow her example and, with an abrupt, violent gesture, pulls off his own identical length of brightly patterned silk, which he then folds—not once, but four times, reducing it to the size of a handkerchief square—and places on top of the vitrine, daring the caretaker to come and fetch it. Such are the hollow refusals, the petty acts of rebellion, to which the vanquished will resort in a futile attempt to prop up the sagging remnants of their dignity.

The caretaker, having retrieved the second of his two prizes—a meaningless concession which costs him nothing—glances about in search of an appropriate repository for the booty and fastens upon a large red lacquered metal bin with a hinged lid, one of Dr. Morgan's trophies, standing nearby against the wall, its glossy surface decorated in the Oriental style by a mountainous terrain peopled with tiny barely discernible figures, some of whom are armed with walking sticks and appear to be attempting to scale the heights, while others have paused and turned their backs to contemplate the daunting magnificence of the landscape. He raises the lid and deposits his plunder inside the container like someone lowering a bucket into the unplumbed depths of a well.

A strangled, gurgling, throaty sound erupts within the cluster of trapped visitors, a sound that resolves itself into a word. "Why!" moans the girl of the mesmerizing stare, less as a question than as a kind of mantra of despair that she repeats at intervals, shaking her head while she struggles to free herself from the bangles encircling her wrist, twisting the bracelet off with a ferocity that leaves behind a red welt, the stubborn angry ghost of the thing she had been wearing. She has the silvery object in her hand now and is examining it, holding it at a distance as if it were something at once dangerous and utterly confounding that demanded careful study. "Why," she says again, more plaintively this time. Her once lethal pale green eyes are glimmering like melting ice, their former potency diffused in a blur of accumulating liquid that keeps threatening to overflow, although not a single tear has fallen yet and possibly never will.

The bearded man pushes his way through the crowd to prevent things going any further, waving his arms about in a peremptory fashion to command everyone's attention. "Stop! Don't do this," he cries, addressing his comrades as the solitary voice of reason in the room. "Don't you realize this lunatic is powerless to keep us here against our will or force us to give up anything at all unless we let him? His success depends entirely on our willingness to collaborate in his crime." The caretaker stands languidly beside his waiting receptacle, observing the effect of this speech with the detached interest of a sports fan, who—to neutralize his stake in the outcome—has placed a large bet on the opposing team. The irate speaker continues his exhortation. "Come on, we're not helpless," he insists. "For god's sake, we have a nine to one advantage. There's nothing to prevent us walking out of here with everything we had when we came in, including our self-respect. If we all just resolve to stand together—if we all refuse to volunteer to become his victims…"

A couple of voices weakly echo this proposition, but even so, pockets are being patted down; handbags have been opened, their contents probed for any suitable offering to substitute in place of whatever the most cherished possessions might actually be. "He wants a boot, does he?" snaps the man in the safari jacket in his querulous voice. "Fine. He'll have it, then." He bends over, propping his lower leg against the opposite knee for balance, grasps the boot by the heel, maneuvers it from side to side, works it free, and hurls it across the floor in the caretaker's direction. When he resumes his upright stance—a bit lopsided now thanks to the inequality of a heavy cotton sock on one foot and the twin of his forfeited boot on the other—he looks oddly satisfied with himself, as if he had just successfully thwarted the authorities by swallowing the contraband. In the midst of this sudden flurry of activity, the girl—ducking her head to avoid any encounter with the others and holding her bangle bracelet between thumb and forefinger like someone disposing of a diseased rodent—makes her way to the open-mouthed canister, dangles the bracelet above it for a moment, and with the hint of a shrug, lets it go, promptly, decisively turning her back, as if all along she had been craving an excuse to be rid of it for good.

The move proves just enough to tip the balance. Like patients at a hospital cafeteria, like sinners at communion, the remaining holdouts fall into line, their carefully chosen objects in hand, and await their turn, one behind the other, to surrender what they're willing to give in exchange for freedom. Some do so in exasperation, yes, some in despair, some almost eagerly, or with feigned indifference, some under protest, or wearily, or spitefully, some chastened by remorse or fear, but regardless of the how or why, all appear at last to have exhausted their attachments. Even the vociferous dissenter, red-faced and still spluttering, ultimately relents and takes his place behind the others.

You might not have expected them to concede so easily, but it has been a long enervating day, full of small shocks, and their will—maybe even their desire—to resist has sunk to its lowest ebb. The price, at this point, looks cheap enough. Besides, to allow oneself to be lured into battle to defend a cuff link or a belt or wristwatch (however precious, however irreplaceable)—to stubbornly insist upon some petty right of ownership in the face of such a determined, unpredictable opponent—seems now an act of madness in itself, one that might almost make the man confronting them look sane by contrast. They have become, at least for the moment, as intent on sacrifice as any would-be saint.

The caretaker, head cocked to one side, holds out an open palm—the scarred one, which feels nothing—and waits to receive them and their offerings, studying with the disquieting tenderness of a healer the wreckage of each face as it approaches. Sometimes he even touches them, brushing an exposed wrist or forearm ever so lightly, almost by accident, with his fingertips. He takes what he is given and examines it, turning it over in his hands, acquainting himself with its shape, its surfaces and its dimensions before somberly nodding his approval and lowering it into the receptacle's growing collection. The cowboy boot of fine-tooled leather, which he has rescued, stands upright, empty, beside his left leg. The ritual of surrender takes place in silence. Maybe this is what they came for after all: to be relieved—whether by force or subterfuge—of something they no longer needed, some stale attachment long since faded from passion to mere habit, which nonetheless, until that moment, they could not voluntarily have given up.

No key, as it turns out moments later, had ever been necessary. The claim had merely been a ploy, an empty threat, maybe an impromptu test of faith. Now, as the caretaker—his plunder safely stashed away for future study—stands poised at the door with the departing visitors gathered anxiously at his back, pressuring him merely with the fact of their presence, a couple of swift flourishes of the wrist is all it takes to flip the deadbolt lock counterclockwise, turn the brass knob, and fling the front door open to the world beyond, unceremoniously inviting their departure. He is done.

What confronts them out there is almost blinding. Even

though the sky has grown so choked with clouds as to be virtually cloudless—an impenetrable uninflected pale grey mass that has consumed the sun—blazing particles of sunlight still permeate the atmosphere, still ricochet off scarcely visible walls and glass and pavement, and glare remorselessly into the unprotected faces and defenseless eyes of the nine people who are emerging from the entrance of the building onto the shallow front stoop with escape on their minds. They hesitate there briefly, feeling for their neighbors, grabbing the nearest elbow or leaning on a shoulder for support as they descend the stairs, but upon reaching the sidewalk without mishap, they grow increasingly emboldened by the solid pavement underfoot and soon gain the courage to disperse, careening along the street in all directions, frenzied as ants, dazzled by the alluring vision of the haven that awaits, that unassailable place with all its familiar comforts, the place each once called home.

Perhaps one day, months or maybe years from now, others may come (innocents not unlike themselves, equally curious, equally restive and bemused, craving a little cultural diversion, or merely an excuse to while away an hour or two), others who may discover quite by chance as they wander through the maze of overstuffed display cases and vitrines or gaze intently at the scrupulously labeled contents of a festooned wall—nestled without fanfare there among the ancient tools and weapons and dislocated machine parts, among the miniature figurines and ivory carvings, the faded fabrics and the jewels and bones and coins and bits of broken crockery, among the priceless artifacts and objects d'art—a pair of red-framed sunglasses, the earpiece tips dented by tiny teeth marks, or a slightly tarnished bangle bracelet, or—hanging upside down from its wispy thinning tail—a hank of braided human hair.

Perhaps those future unsuspecting strangers taking note one

day of what they see and pondering the nine abandoned objects and their rightful place within the rest of the collection will ultimately be enough to redeem the sacrifice their visiting predecessors made, but that time will have to wait. Right now—at this particular moment on this bright grey waning summer afternoon and into the foreseeable future until who knows when—the sign that hangs on the Morgan Foundation's obstinate front door says with some finality, in big block letters, CLOSED.

P eace at last. Solitude.

No one to answer to, no one to impress, charm, chastise, care for, enlighten or entertain, no one, that is, at least until tomorrow. The caretaker presses his damp forehead against the cool of the impartial plaster wall. He stays there motionless and listens. In the wake of the recent invasion, there is only silence. The building holds its breath. He holds his, too, and waits. And still no sound.

He has begun again to monitor the passage of time—an old familiar habit to help fend off panic—invoking the reassuring certainty of numbers as they follow each other with inexorable, if meaningless, precision (eleven, twelve, thirteen ...). He pictures the shapes of the numerals, their lines and arcs superimposed in thickening succession one upon the next, blotting out everything that came before. The sequence of syllables composes a rhythmic nonsense nursery rhyme in his head while he counts out the seconds to himself like a junkie compulsively postponing the relief of his next fix: sixty makes one minute, and then sixty more makes two, and after two will soon come three. Is he hastening time by means of this ritual, or retarding it? Or is he just fiddling helplessly, irrelevantly, on the sidelines until the inevitable arrives and overtakes him?

At last, just when he thinks he can bear it no longer, something shudders briefly somewhere down below, a tremulous stuttering gulp—the protest of a faulty pipe, perhaps—but as spontaneously as it erupts, it dies away, leaving him to wonder if he really heard it after all, or if it were instead some random auditory hallucination conjured out of nothingness by hope. More silence. The noisy irreverent departure of the nine unwelcome visitors—the latest trespassers to violate the place with his permission and defile the sanctity of its private places with their strange voices and their strange indifferent eyes—is not even an echo anymore. How much longer must this cruel, protracted game go on before his most recent transgression will have earned forgiveness? And still he waits, head bowed, still motionless, still scarcely breathing now, while his sweaty, burning forehead pressed into the wall congeals itself there, obliterating any palpable distinction between flesh and plaster.

And then, at last, it happens. His forbearance is rewarded. The thing he has been longing for occurs. With a sudden tremor, the whole building, all three stories of it, exhales, heaves a long, low sigh, and settling a little deeper into its foundations like a luxuriating drowsy cat, surrenders. Everything it has been withholding from him, it now releases.

Close by, within what might have been a hollow space inside the wall, something shifts, dislodges itself, scuttles its way downward a short distance and comes to rest again, clunk. At the same moment, a windowpane rattles in its frame—precipitated by a wayward breeze, the voice of reason would insist, pedantically, by way of explanation (thereby explaining, in fact, nothing.) Another rattles in reply. A third joins in, making a noisy rattling opinionated chorus of impatient glass, agitating for freedom. The draft that might allegedly have caused all this, as if fortified by its success, moves on now, disturbing curtains, rustling other loosened fabrics along the way as it goes from room to room, probing every corner, and slinks upstairs. An isolated floorboard creaks somewhere above his head. Things stretch themselves, expanding and contracting, emitting groans and whines and low-pitched whispers. From the rear of the building comes a hiss like steam escaping—but it is summertime, or hovering on the brink of autumn, if you insist; at any rate, there is no steam. Without warning, something upstairs falls to the carpet with a thud but does not seem to break.

Blame gravity. Blame an erratic movement of the air. Blame condensation or decay. Blame what you like: the whole place has come alive again and has found its voice and is chattering away in its native language to the solitary listener, the secret language he alone in his devout apprenticeship has had the patience to begin to comprehend. Such a riot of competing sounds tantalize his ears—familiar sounds that have scarcely any names and, being nameless, may be alleged by the outsiders not to exist at all except perhaps in their pathetic onomatopoetic approximations: the pings and thwacks and clicks and plops and sizzles a jealous human tongue attempts in vain to emulate. The caretaker, seeking to lend encouragement by keeping up his end of things, ventures a few bars of his tuneless whistle and, moments later, receives in answer a wheezing groan, as if an idle motor in a distant room had spontaneously started up again.

Slowly raising his head, he gingerly separates his forehead from the damp discolored patch of plaster against which it has been resting, unwittingly retaining as he does so—but no matter, there is no one there to see—a whitened smudge like ash upon his brow that mirrors the stain of sweat he has left behind blistered upon the wall, commingling the DNA of man and building. The caretaker is almost smiling now. He insinuates a moistened fingertip into the tiny opening in the newly wounded wall, just far enough to remove a bit of exposed plaster dust, which he tests on the tip of his tongue, sampling its chalky bitterness. There are plenty of scars to be explored. Closing his eyes to concentrate his senses, he traces several of the meandering fissures of cracked paint etched into the uneven pebbled surface of the wall, almost caressing them, not so much to heal them as to know them.

For a while he lingers there in the anteroom, still listening, still touching things, breathing in the reassuring fragrance of stale air, gradually eradicating his recent estrangement from the place. Then, bending over, he unties the laces and removes, first his shoes, then Dr. Morgan's silky chartreuse socks, which he rolls together into a single ball and slips inside the monogrammed breast pocket of the Charvet shirt. With the shoes tucked securely under his arm, he heads back toward the first gallery on his way upstairs. The soles of his feet, indifferent to the risk of splinters, deliberately scuff along the floor, reacquainting themselves with its familiar flaws and subtle undulations. One by one, he turns out lights as he goes. Darkness trails after him.

If this were actually the end—and perhaps it is, although no one seems to know it yet—then whatever comes next amounts to no more than an epilogue.

The following day, August 29, is—or would have been—Dr. Morgan's ninety-first birthday. In keeping with the long-standing Foundation tradition, an evening of celebrations was scheduled to mark the occasion. By mid-afternoon the caterers would arrive and begin their preparations. Furniture in the third-floor study would be uprooted from its accustomed place, maneuvered into corners and covered with protective cloths creating mounds of ghostly silhouettes, or stored away along with various vulnerable items of memorabilia in other nearby rooms behind locked doors for safekeeping. Three dozen folding chairs, rented for the occasion, would be delivered and arranged symmetrically six rows deep to accommodate the anticipated overflow of invited guests forecast by the unprecedented success of the previous year's event. Two distinguished academics with widely divergent views had been selected to provide the entertainment by reading from their as yet unpublished papers on the impact of the Morgan legacy and engaging in a brief moderated discussion that, given the nature of the participants, promised to be heated enough to hold the audience's attention while still maintaining the required aura of civility. Afterwards cocktails and hors d'oeuvres were to be served, accompanied by toasts to the absent honoree. The caretaker—who had from time to time on previous occasions managed to insinuate himself into an inconspicuous spot near the back of the room from which to witness the festivities—prided himself on being a member of the servant class and was once again, as usual, pointedly omitted from the list of invitees.

Loose ends. No matter how long the night, it won't be long enough to do what must be done. Who knows, night may have come already, be it only the perpetual night of windowless rooms, of closets where he had spent a good part of his child-hood crouched behind the drooping weary musty clothes with all their musty secrets. At any rate, oblivious to the state of things in the outside world, the barefoot man has now method-ically retraced his steps, as if doing so might magically reverse the past. Once more he penetrates the depths of the building and once more ascends the stairs, moving slowly, purposefully, making each step count. Haste would only breed carelessness and be of no avail. He watches his right hand gliding up along the banister the way it had more than a dozen times each day since that first rainy afternoon before his interview, before the commitment, before the wound. The longer he studies its rep-tilian progress, the more alien it becomes. His palm performs a kind of incidental cleansing action in the process, absorbing the day's accretions, the sweat and smudgy fingerprints left be-hind upon the surface by all those careless strangers who had come and gone. What had once been part of them is part of him now.

He makes his way past the familiar landmarks: the forlorn reproachful plinth still waiting for something to display, the Dürer portrait with its single watchful eye, incapable of actually seeing anything yet equally incapable of letting anything get by it unobserved. In a remote corner of the second floor, the time-pieces—some mute, others only barely audible—go on bemoan-ing, each in its own idiosyncratic way, the incessant seepage of time. The rhythm of his heartbeat listens and, with nothing better to obey, joins in. Time, in fact, is catching up with him. If there were such a thing as mandatory retirement around here, it would long since have made him obsolete. Already he is one year older than the dead man ever got to be.

The study door remains ajar the way the hasty departure of its recent visitors had left it. The room is beckoning. A pale shaft of lamplight from inside oozes out along the hall carpet, blanching a sliver of its ornate pattern and turning the voluptuous red roses pictured on it an unearthly pink. Such are the stratagems by means of which the building has contrived to plead, complain, seduce, and make known its needs. Right now, of course, the place is teeming with demands on his attention, but none so urgent as the one directly up ahead. Unfortunately, he only manages to make it halfway down the corridor to his intended destination before an apparition startles him and arrests his progress.

On the west wall, a few feet from the entrance to the study, hangs an oval gilt framed mirror, the dimmed surface of its glass tarnished and speckled with opacities, within which a face has just materialized that is staring back at him, relentless and unblinking. Despite the oblique angle of his view as he stands there transfixed by what he sees, despite the incidental mottling of the complexion and slight distortion of the features engendered by the imperfections in the glass, despite the superficial lack of resemblance to, for example, the picture on his recently expired passport, the image he is now looking at in disbelief nonetheless purports to be his own reflection. Its perfect stillness immobilizes him, as if it were actually the original and he no more than a poor mimic, the creature of its whims, incapable of any action it does not initiate. The raised eyebrow hints at mockery. Is he really smiling, or is that just a shadow transfiguring the corner of the mouth?

Several minutes pass before he manages to disentangle himself from the delusion: the face he is confronting in the mirror is not, in fact, the one he has learned to call his own, the one that he recalls from his shave that morning, the one with the sunken cheeks, the one whose flesh his fingers press aside to rescue from the blade as it glides treacherously upwards along his Adam's apple. No, it is the face of the Other, a face he knows at least as well and—thanks to the myriad portraits he has been contemplating on a daily basis for years—possibly better than his own. How could he have failed to recognize it? And given the frequency of his journeys along this very route, how could he have failed to encounter the phenomenon before?

Directly opposite the study door, catty-corner to the mirror, hangs the twin of the image he had unaccountably mistaken for himself. It is a black and white portrait of Dr. Morgan, probably made when the man was in his early sixties, one of those posed, formal, close-up photographs that employ an exaggerated chiaroscuro as a means of dramatizing the importance of the subject. The raised eyebrow, the subtle suggestion of a smile, the look of irony—these are merely the defensive measures of a sophisticate attempting, not entirely successfully, to signal his detachment from the process and divorce himself from the cliché. If what the caretaker had been looking at was a reflection of Morgan's image then, according to the laws of physics, Morgan had been looking back at him and somewhere in the mirror, unbeknownst to either, their gazes must have met.

The caretaker summons the courage to tear himself away from this crisis of identities and enters the study. A cloying perfume, the last vestige of the invasion, taints the air, mingling with the smell of stale cigar. He makes a cursory survey of the room. Everything remains more or less as he had arranged it that morning in anticipation of his visitors, but since they had—

admittedly by invitation—not merely looked but also touched, objects have shifted slightly or been moved, if only by a fraction of an inch, from their intended positions, and to the eye of the connoisseur this amounts to a state of chaos: he might as well have been contemplating a room turned upside down.

He removes from under his arm the shoes he has been carrying and places them near the hearth beside Dr. Morgan's embroidered velvet slippers, into which he gingerly insinuates his naked feet. Being some two sizes too large, his feet protrude out the back, squashing down the heels with every step as he shuffles across the carpet to the center casement window behind Morgan's desk. He turns the handle and—after a bit of effort against the resistance built up for nearly a quarter century that has calcified a desire to remain sealed shut—succeeds in pushing open the reluctant window, admitting a gust of damp night city air along with a small winged creature that circles the room, whining like a miniature helicopter, and then secretes itself behind a book on one of the upper shelves. The room inhales with a gasp, as if it had been holding its breath all these years, thirsting for the relief of a little contamination.

Following this daring act of sacrilege, the caretaker retrieves the stub of his purloined cigar from the ashtray, mouths the tip experimentally before managing to get it lit again, coughs twice, and takes a seat at the desk. Hidden in plain sight among the casually arrayed papers in front of him is a large unsealed, unaddressed manila envelope from which he removes several sheets of pale blue notepaper, yellowing slightly at the edges, and monogrammed—like the breast pocket of the chartreuse shirt he is wearing—with a flamboyant *M*, embraced on either side by the subservient initials *C* and *A*. The top sheet of paper—two thirds of it consumed by the large, loopy script Morgan had set about developing late in life on the advice of his personal graphologist to accentuate certain desirable character-istics latent in his nature—is dated August 29, 1987, and begins as follows:

> *To my dear wife, to my loyal friends, faithful enemies, and whomever else it may concern,*
>
> *I am not, as you must know, a superstitious man, but sud-denly this afternoon, realizing to my profound astonishment that I have just become the same age my father was the day he died (and despite the fact that I fully intend to do my very best to outlast all of you, if not actually to live forever) as I con-template the prospect of yet another challenging trip abroad in a few months' time the pernicious desire*

The caretaker takes up the reading glasses lying poised be-side the open dictionary and, fitting them onto the bridge of his nose, waggles his head about as he adjusts to the sudden improvement in his vision. He reads on.

> *the pernicious desire to take stock grows increasingly difficult to suppress. Birthdays will do that to a man sometimes, divert the healthiest of minds down a maze of philosophical blind alleys. Memories invade my dreams. (Or is it the reverse?) Ghosts point fingers.*

Here, abruptly, the writing ends. The caretaker takes another tentative puff on the cigar, leans back in his chair, and looks over the top of the rimless glasses, as if contemplating a troublesome spot near the corner of the ceiling. Then, suddenly, in a quick, decisive motion, he snatches up the letter, crumples it into a ball and tosses it toward the middle of the room. This action reveals another, similar sheet of stationery, bearing the identical date. Many of the words are different; the gist, however, is the same.

> *My dearest Helen,*
> *You have never asked for explanations and I owe you*

none. We have lived too long in peace through silences, our long judicious silences, and peacefully apart. Why spoil it now merely to put down things you probably already know and might prefer to pretend you didn't. But tonight for the first time I feel my age (or someone's age) as a terminal affliction. Am I really now the same age my father was the year he died? Not that I'm a superstitious man (as you know all too well having reserved that part of the equation for yourself) but in the end, whether it be this year, next year, or decades from now, one must eventually surrender the exhilarating burden of a secret life to the ravages of posthumous reputation. At that point, others take charge. Thanks to your proximity, at least in a strictly legal sense, they will surely come to you. They will besiege you with questions to which you have no answers. You will need to be prepared. Be ready to lie and, most of all, to believe in what you say.

Again the letter stops unfinished and this one, too, the caretaker discards in the same manner as the first before reaching for the dried-up fountain pen and refilling it at the inkstand. An unblemished sheet of stationery is now confronting him. He scrutinizes it as if he were reading an invisible message intended for his eyes alone. Rotating his left wrist like an athlete limbering up for some strenuous activity, he begins to write, producing a large voluptuous *A* followed seamlessly by a few additional flourishes, forming the word *August.* This proves to be as liberating as if he had suddenly awakened from a spell—or fallen prey to one. All hesitation ceases. The fluency of Morgan's imperious penmanship takes over:

My one and only Helen (and anyone else who cares, or with whom you choose to share what I'm about to tell),

Not to make too much of the occasion, but on this my 66th birthday, being temporarily afflicted to the point of near incapacity by that old turbulence in the gut (a clash between eagerness and dread, no doubt) which always accompanies the prospect of revisiting the familiar distant place where I must soon once more be going, it may be timely to address the looming question of posterity. After all, it seems I have a reputation to uphold. Or, preferably perhaps, one to destroy. In either case, I fear a great responsibility may one day fall upon your narrow shoulders.

Looking back, which as you know I am always loath to do, and assuming I have what's called a conscience and that it happened to need clearing up, I could hazard the confessional mode and begin by saying I was responsible for as many as three deaths. That would of necessity include the suicide, although to presume to hold oneself accountable for such an independent solitary act seems an unforgivable affront to the sublime autonomy of the perpetrator and is nothing but sheer megalomania. On the other hand, I did know the boy, there's no denying that, and merely knowing him all those many years ago, given who I am, may be enough to implicate me in his story if that turned out to be the version he preferred. From time to time of an evening when the work was done we would fall into conversation and explore at length the usual important subjects which were certain to have included thoughts on death because after all, what meaning does life have without it. But that was only words. As to the rest, it is impossible to say at this distance which of us may have been the victim and which of us the predatory innocent. We both survived.

The accident was another matter. That was long before you, back in those dear dark days when, although certainly no minor, I was nonetheless still young enough to be presumed relatively innocent in the eyes of the law and since, contrary to what would have been my preference, an accident of birth had saddled me with all the additional advantages of race and class and gender, not to mention certain innate talents,

He has come to the bottom of the page. He turns it over and continues on the other side. The words inscribed on the front show through the thin blue paper ever so faintly, reversed, illegible, like prescient ghosts as he writes over them.

the random acts of carelessness I happened to commit were usually passed off as mere indiscretions and almost automatically granted absolution. [Such are the indulgences that fail to build character, although an excess of what passes for good fortune isn't really much of an alibi.]

Up until that night, which was the last time I got behind the wheel of a car, I would have rated myself a pretty decent driver despite a susceptibility to distraction as I navigated my thoughts or my immediate surroundings. At any rate, there was a lot of rain. The neighborhood was unfamiliar. The roads were dark and treacherous. Visibility was poor. The report said so. When some fluttery agitated white thing suddenly shot out of nowhere some hundred feet ahead, looking like a flock of startled birds battering at each other with their wings, there was nothing to be done. Given the speed of the car, the speed of the moving creature and the rapidly shrinking distance between us, contact was inevitable. Besides, before the car could stop, the woman stopped, stood there drenched in her flimsy bathrobe in the road and turned in my direction. Just before impact, my headlights showed her face to me. She was smiling eerily like someone greeting an unexpected but very welcome visitor whom she hadn't dared to hope to see again. The woman was no stranger. We had been almost friends at school. Logically, of course, the headlights must have been blinding. Still, I can't help but think she somehow knew that it was me who was about to hit her. She looked content. Maybe she was happy to have found just anyone to do it for her. By the time I managed to reach her after the collision as she lay there crumpled in the road, her left arm outstretched at an impossible angle reaching for something and her face burrowed into the asphalt, a dark stain was oozing out across the dirty wet white cloth beneath her. Of course my mind grasped the horror, but what I SAW—there is no euphemistic way to put it—what I saw was BEAUTIFUL. I mean hopelessly, undeniably, mesmerizingly beautiful. Those are the facts. I can't help it. No point pretending otherwise. That is who I am.

There was loss of consciousness. Injuries on both sides.

The caretaker takes another sheet of stationery, puts a number 3 in the top left corner and without hesitation continues writing. As he sits hunched over Morgan's desk, the damp evening air sneaks in the open window, disturbing the hair at the back of his neck like a neglected lover, greedy for attention.

Only hers were fatal, according to the autopsy that is, which determined, in addition to the cause of death, not simply that there were opiates in her system, but that she was also six weeks pregnant. My previous acquaintance with the victim naturally aroused the suspicion of the authorities and complicated matters. I don't blame them. Had I been drinking (which thanks to some undeserved stroke of luck I hadn't, because that would have been entirely normal for me at the time) the consequences would undoubtedly have been a lot more serious. As it was, after weighing all the circumstances, the investigation ultimately concluded I was not culpable. One tragic accident. Two dead. In the end, thanks in part to the intervention of my father (with whom I was still on speaking terms) and his powers of persuasion, the record was effectively expunged.

I suppose for the ordinary person, questions of guilt might be expected to arise, but guilt is merely hubris in disguise and exists only to provide the impotent with some pathetic illusion of power, something to hide behind and beg forgiveness for and, in that way, obtain permission to forget. No wonder adolescents wallow in it. For those of us who have befriended chaos and accept how little blame or credit we have any right to claim for what becomes of others (and maybe even of our-

selves), guilt is one of the many luxuries we need to have the courage to renounce.

But enough of narrative. Enough of specious explanations. Enough philosophy. Besides, I have undoubtedly done worse. Death is not the only way to wreck a life, as you could probably attest. So much for remorse. And now consider this: what if everything I just confessed never really even happened?

The caretaker, pen at the ready, awaiting further instructions, finds himself once more at a loss for words. Decades of apprenticeship lurk in the wings eager to reward him. He has of course read the journals, all forty-two of them, once straight through from beginning to end over six days during the first phase of his employment, bathing himself in the idiosyncrasies of their syntax until he almost began to mistake it for his own; and then again—in what has cumulatively amounted to a second time—governed by the self-imposed rigorous bedtime ritual that entailed not merely reading each entry, not merely mouthing its words aloud as if he were reciting a catechism, but copying them out, one by one into a set of corresponding journals, reliving the other life as he transcribed it, and inadvertently mimicking in the process the continuous evolution of Morgan's penmanship. There are two sets of journals now, identical in content, virtually identical in appearance, the existence of each a challenge to the authenticity of the other. Only one has been allowed to remain behind in the guise of the original, locked away inside the cabinet with the leaded glass doors, while its twin, slated for destruction, languishes in a shallow grave at the back of a vacant lot some half a dozen miles away awaiting the inevitability of the unwitting bulldozers that will pulverize its pages and mulch its words into extinction in the sacred name of progress.

Dozens of such unmarked burial plots now punctuate the city, harboring their precious contraband. Several stolen treasures reside in individual sealed containers fathoms deep beneath the indifferent river, which is always moving on; some occupy small crevices in old stone walls while others decay complacently behind the loosened tiles of public urinals or under mounds of garbage in the great municipal dump. The dead letter office in accordance with its duty retains, among the countless other items of undeliverable mail, three unclaimed packages, each wrapped in butcher paper and bearing the handwritten address of somewhere that does not exist, without any indication of where it might have come from. Certain objects lie hidden in plain sight: an engraved gold wedding band lost amid the contents of a thrift shop's overcrowded jewelry case, a rusty tire iron in the husk of an abandoned burned-out car, an ancient Egyptian coin embedded in a patch of sidewalk. By means of these surreptitious installations, their subversive curator—in a series of unsanctioned expeditions conducted in his free time at odd hours of the day or night over the course of the past decade—has staked his claim. The Morgan seeds are sown. Chance will now be left to govern their fate and determine which, if any, shall find a worthy savior who will help it to bear fruit.

Supporting the weight of his forehead with the thumb and forefinger of his right hand pressed against his temple, the caretaker is studying the page before him, as if hoping to lure from its remaining empty space the blessing of another sentence. *History is my religion. I have given it my life,* he writes, then with a single line through the middle of the ten words, crosses it out and begins again:

> *In the wake of any absence, nagging questions will naturally arise. A sudden void aches to be filled. If Nature abhors a vacuum, human nature contrives to find it unendurable, so I believe I do not flatter myself overmuch to presume that sooner or later they will seek you out, the maggots we po-*

litely call the writers, the biographers, the critics, journalists, theorists and historians and whatever else they may purport to be, selectively amassing information in support of some predetermined point of view they have already sanctioned as the truth. They will come to you because, in spite of all the people I have known and even loved (recklessly, after my fashion) and the ones who have loved me (occasionally the same people, seldom at the same time) so few real friends remain. You are the best that's left to tell the tales; you have the best credentials.

Posterity is looming up ahead, ready to assume whatever shape it's given. You might ask why we should care, we non-believers, for whom the end of us might just as well constitute the end of everything. But vanity is made of hardy stuff. Long after the heart quits its incessant pumping, after the blood stops flowing, allowing gravity to have its way, after the brain has managed to forget all it once knew and can forget no more, when the postmortem seizures finally subside and give up simulating life, still the old insatiable helpless home-less ego lingers on in the ether, guarding its exposed flanks against the impending facile summings-up.

So I write to ask you—beg you, if I must—to save me. No, not ME *exactly, for I'll no longer really matter then, but everything I gave my life to along with the empty shell of the idea of me that bears my name. It will of course take cunning. It will take discipline. You must be willing to relinquish your lifelong infatuation with those curious illusions you mistake for facts and are continually defending against the skeptics. Whatever you may know of me, or think you have surmised, keep to yourself. Allow the thing to flourish while it can, like a precious hothouse plant inside the airless vault of your memory. When they come to pry open your sealed lips with their ingratiating smiles and disarmingly blunt questions, offering you as a bribe whatever they can summon in the way of charm and earnest, witty conversational gambits, seasoned every now and then with unsolicited disclosures to induce you to respond in kind, don't put up a fight. Feed them everything they want until they choke on it. What they spit out is what the world will swallow.*

Of course, as they will surely tell you, they only want to get the story right, but evil is the inevitable firstborn child of that sanctimonious monster known as good intentions and I am no one's story. So let me be instead the rapist they are looking for, the murderer, the plagiarist, the thief, the fraud. Collaborate. Help them to explain me into nonexistence. Help them make me disappear. Save me by condemnation, obfuscation, misdirection. Lie about me. Indict me. Contradict me. Libel me. Defame me. Slander me. Stigmatize me. Save me from the consuming world. Let me be. Let falsehood be my shroud.

And when at last you weary of deceit and can invent no longer, you have permission to withdraw and abandon them to their agonies of thwarted curiosity. Let them interrogate STUFF for answers if, confusing the accumulation of information with understanding, they think they must know more. It may not be the lurid confession they were hoping for, the secret diary or memoir, or that ever so subtly self-justifying concoction, the autobiography, with its tangle of false leads and failed promises, but everything I am is in there undisguised, apparent to anyone who really wants to see. True, I am nothing but the hapless author of the book; I'm not its subject. And yet that is precisely why, as the servant of a better master than myself, I lie before the reader naked on its pages.

What is it that your Bible tries to tell us the man said when he returned from being gone and the weeping woman recognized him? Was it, Don't touch me? Touching is forbidden? Was it, Stop clinging to me? Sounds like a seduction, don't you think? A challenge in the form of a perverse invitation to transgress. NOLI ME TANGERE doesn't get us any closer, since Latin was not his native language and those could not have been his actual words, but merely a rough translation from yet another language he did not speak, presuming that he spoke at all after he died. We have good reason to doubt everything. The reporter is no eyewitness. He has relied on gossip, twisted, modified and reshaped in accordance with his prescribed agenda: to cow the doubters out there into a state of blind belief. If we know anything at all, we know that different words have different meanings, not to mention the deep-rooted evocations buried in their forgotten histories and derivations. Translators have no choice but to take liberties and make compromises, but no approximation can pretend to be the thing itself any more than an object's name supplants its physical reality or metaphor can substitute for fact. Words themselves in any language are merely poor approximations of the elusive fleeting thoughts. In the end, the goal is silence. Alas, we may need words to get there.

The letter has consumed the better part of five pages. The writer pauses, then appends a valediction, followed by the symbolic flourish of a signature: *Yours as always, in absentia, Charles.* But this is not the last word. Apparently there remains a postscript to be written. He observes with the mild interest of a stranger the movement of his left hand. He watches the pen he is holding form letters and the letters assemble themselves into words. Two words: *Burn this,* it says. And moments later, obedient as always, he does so.

Meanwhile, as the small conflagration savors its ration of crushed paper and slowly, gradually, under the supervision of its creator, consumes it, a broken thing sequestered somewhere up above waits for its redemption.

C entered on the roof of the three-story red brick building that houses the Society for the Preservation of the Legacy of Dr. Charles Alexander Morgan, set back just far enough to prevent it being visible from the street below, to satisfy the requirements of the Landmarks Commission (an agency that despite its vehement opposition to the intrusion of offensive anachronisms, tended to equate the unseen with the nonexistent), stands a rudimentary twenty by thirty-foot rectilinear structure roughly ten feet high sheathed in corrugated metal siding with a narrow door at the rear and a single window on each of its three remaining sides. It had been erected some five years before Dr. Morgan's death in anticipation of the future necessity of providing the building's staunchly independent resident with some kind of nonintrusive live-in help, someone who, in the guise of secretary, archivist, or research assistant, could nonetheless be prevailed upon to run the occasional domestic errand, provide a little companionship for a restless semi-invalid, and should the need ultimately arise, do a bit of basic nursing as well. Given Dr. Morgan's apparently unimpeachable good health, interrupted only by his sudden demise, the structure's intended purpose as servants quarters had remained unfulfilled—at least, that is, until twenty-four years ago when the caretaker moved in, thereby belatedly supplying a reason for its existence.

As an experienced nomad reluctant to make his own indelible mark on a situation which, even as the days and months and years went by, he continued to regard as temporary, he has left things essentially the way he found them when he first arrived. In spite of the studious application of a fresh coat of paint from time to time, the room remains the same anemic shade of yellow it was then, with the same outdated stove and sink and fridge lining the south wall, a bathroom and adjoining closet to the east, and an entrance consisting of an opening in the floor that resembles a hatch without a lid, enclosed on three sides by a metal railing.

No interior walls intrude upon the space. No pictures threaten to betray the occupant's personal history or predilections, that is, unless of course you choose to place in that category a series of obscure mathematical notations inscribed in a remote unlit corner near the entrance, or the large detailed map of the city taped up for years beside one window, its surface veined with red and blue and purple intersecting pencil pathways punctuated by asterisks, indications (one might reasonably surmise) of the places where a diligent explorer had once been or had once hoped to go. The map itself is gone now. Only its rectangular ghost—a fresher, paler patch of yellow than that of the surrounding surface—remains behind, the residue of a recent absence.

Lined up against the wall, underneath a succession of hooks for various items of discarded clothing (last week's workshirt, a wide-brimmed leather hat, a pair of brown corduroys suspended by a belt loop dangling limp, lopsided empty legs) stand four pairs of shoes, toes against the baseboard, as if four docile prisoners awaiting execution had suddenly evaporated, leaving only their footwear for the firing squad.

The furnishings are minimal: a long pine dining table with a complement of mismatched chairs parallels the open kitchen, doubling—according to need—as either desk or workbench, while a monastic iron bed, situated directly beneath a modest skylight, provides the chronic insomniac, who spends most of his nights there, a mesmerizing nocturnal spectacle of infinitely nuanced shifting shades of darkness, punctuated only on rare occasions by a glimpse of moon or of a last surviving pair of fading stars. No moon tonight. No stars. Nothing to temper the intractability of night except whatever happens to issue from the disconsolate streetlamps down below or from the occasional lighted window in one of the surrounding towers, offering its chilly spectacle of intimacy to random strangers across the way.

The caretaker has entered the room, his refuge, and having blindly navigated familiar obstacles, is standing perfectly still in his ill-fitting borrowed slippers, immobilized midway between bed and closet, as if mentally rehearsing that which might come next. At last, apparently satisfied with what he has mapped out, he makes his way over to the closet, opens the door, and feels along the front edge of the shelf, gently insinuating his fingertips underneath a stack of freshly laundered shirts which he removes and, keeping the stack perfectly intact, places at one end of the dining table. The maneuver exposes—beside a couple of leather pouches and various implements of a somewhat surgical nature—a lumpy mound of blue cloth tucked into a far corner of the closet shelf. The caretaker is there to retrieve it.

All this he has managed by feel alone. Only when he has the bundle safely positioned on the table does he reach up and pull the chain to turn on the overhead light and permit himself to examine what lies before him. He unwraps the blue shroud, carefully, reverently, almost reluctantly, peeling back one shabby layer at a time like someone dismembering an origami bird, doing his best to delay what has finally become an inevitable confrontation with his old nemesis. Once uncovered, sharp translucent edges glint at him in a manner easily mistaken for malevolence. The two hundred and forty-seven broken shards of Morgan's artifact have bit by bit been reassembled and made into a whole again, or if not exactly whole, at least into a single object. Of course, like anything attempting to disguise the scars of time or of experience and emulate that which it once was but is no longer, the restoration has its flaws. Each fragment fits together with its neighbors as it did when they were one, but what had been seamless then, now simply isn't, quite. Here and there, despite the rehabilitating surgeon's vigilance, minute vitreous traces of dried glue betray a join. The occasional gap mars previously smooth expanses. Although nearly identical to the original in size and shape, material, and in component parts, the thing sadly turns out to be no better than an imperfect version of its former self, much as Dr. Frankenstein's doomed creation, likewise assembled out of disparate parts, proved to be, although undoubtedly a living, breathing creature, only very imperfect as a human. In fact, it is precisely the proximity to success in this instance that accentuates the failure. Nonetheless, in spite of these minor, virtually imperceptible shortcomings, an untrained eye indifferent to such subtleties and unacquainted with the imponderable magnificence of what once existed would probably be willing to accept this fastidiously mended thing as Dr. Morgan's original unadulterated phenomenon of Nature.

The caretaker slowly circles the table, bending over every now and then with his head on one side as he does so to study the results of his work from all angles, imagining how a prospective viewer might judge it and, thanks to a willful disregard of the tyrannical perfectionist in his nature, finds it good, or more precisely, good enough, at least given the present circumstances and the exigencies of time. He lifts the object to his chest, maneuvering it until he has it balanced, albeit somewhat precariously, across his forearms, secured there by the cradle of his fingers and, while still refusing to relinquish the impediment of the slippers, begins his halting shuffling treacherous progress down the stairs toward the vacant plinth whose emptiness, like a mark of shame, remains half hidden in the shadowy corner on the second floor to which it has been relegated since the incident that robbed it of its prize.

It is a deliberate but unceremonious reunion. With painstaking care, so as not to accidentally undo what he has so painstakingly accomplished, the caretaker, leaving the plinth undisturbed in its place, slowly eases the burden by degrees from his outstretched arms onto the smooth dark surface which gleams enticingly even in the absence of any decent lighting. The small flattened portion of what may be called the object's underside (although in actuality it has no sides to speak of)—a feature apparently intrinsic to its original formation, as if its ultimate destination had been foreordained—comes in contact once again with the top of the plinth on which it used to sit so proudly and cleaves to it; they cleave to one another. A halfhearted attempt to make adjustments meets resistance. Of course, it may be nothing more than friction holding them in place, or gravity, or maybe some intractable sense of rightness acting as a magnet, insisting that as they are now, they must remain. Or could it be that after the protracted separation they have just endured, coming together once again is enough to reignite the dormant embers of their respective natures, generating sufficient heat to melt the two antithetical solids so that they congeal into a single entity, incapable of ever being sundered without irreparable damage to them both.

At any rate, they have been reunited now: the one wrested from the earth, the other, half celestial. The artifact sits poised at an angle on its perch, inclined slightly forward with the tips of its outer leaves (including the one, now cleansed of blood, that punctured the caretaker's palm) curled back upon themselves, as if to proffer the intricate crystalline folds of its complex interior for the inspection of anyone who ventures up the staircase to the second floor and gains the landing. Equilibrium has been restored: reality no longer contradicts the promise written on the label. Dürer's inscrutable woman sees all and makes no judgment.

Little now remains for his final tour of inspection before retiring but to test a few locked doors, set the alarms, close an open window, put objects back where they belong, to finally return things to the way that they were always meant to be. The braided rope with its cautionary one-word proclamation has been reattached, barring access by those who will come later to the private third-floor rooms where the caretaker has gone to complete his mission. As he moves down the corridor between the walls, soundlessly, like a figment of his own imagination, the air makes way for him to pass and closes up behind him, eradicating any trace of his passage. The house submits.

Autumn has come early. The days remain warm and humid, even when the breeze blows hard, and yet already leaves, still green but curling inward on themselves, forsake their branches, littering the gutters and clogging grates. Gulls desert the river and venture inland, their cries sounding the emergency. Three solitary doomed flies, having come in at the open window seeking refuge, regret their achievement and grow desperate, buzzing for a way out, dashing themselves unsuccessfully against the windowpane that lures them with the bright inaccessible image of a world they had just managed to escape.

The caretaker stands naked, a glass in hand, before the uncompromising expanse of Dr. Morgan's bathroom mirror, in which, on daily visits, he has been observing what he thinks of as his progress, watching himself gradually, almost imperceptibly, changing, growing older, growing old. He makes a methodical study of the reflection, as if committing it to memory so he will recognize it in case they meet again: the naturally unruly hair, colorless as a moth's wing and usually too wispy for gravity to tame, still furrowed by the morning's combing and pomaded into place; the convoluted creases of a troubled forehead; the narrow flinty pale grey eyes confronting him with imponderable questions about what it is they see; the patrician angularity of the nose; the almost lipless mouth inclining upward at the outer edges, as if helplessly aspiring to a smile. He lowers his gaze—past flesh sagging from its own weight, past the Adam's apple (like a peach pit lodged inside the throat), the prominent clavicles—and lets it linger over the rhythmic expansion and contraction of the solar plexus. He runs a finger over his ribs to make certain he exists, tallying up their number (a reassuring twelve in all). The white hairs on his chest encircle each nipple and trace two thin uninterrupted lines joined at the sternum that descend as one, like a harbinger of the coroner's incision at the commencement of an autopsy, dividing left from right, and bisecting the navel in a downward journey toward the pubis.

A phalanx of some two dozen pill bottles, like an army of toy soldiers on the march, interrupt the view, occupying much of the marble vanity that runs the width of the mirror, their contents—at least according to the labels bearing Dr. Morgan's name—already decades out of date, calling into question the efficacy of what they have to offer. The caretaker whispers the names aloud, so much Latin, so much less Greek, as if the sounds alone might be intoxicating. There are those with only modest goals, intended to do no more than help maintain the body's status quo or help postpone the next calamity it might be prone to; those whose only purpose is to counteract unwanted side effects. Others foster sleep or wakefulness, even euphoria, while several merely dull the pain, wherever it may be, thereby making way for new sensations, or the new experience of feeling almost nothing. Some, of course, are even more ambitious, precipitating altered states of consciousness or implicitly promising to resurrect the past by restoring the power of weakened faculties or of those threatening extinction. As a patient, the Doctor, full of curiosity like most committed men of science, had clearly been an adventurous consumer of medications, eager to use his body as a private laboratory in which to explore whatever new experience it might be artificially induced to undergo.

Various implements of personal grooming keep the drugs company on the counter: an unsanitized toothbrush and crimped toothpaste tube resting in a tumbler, an ancient safety razor, sharpened blade intact ("the very blade that grazed the Morgan cheek morning after morning for so many years," the caretaker might have said to his assembled visitors had they ever made it this far), along with an assortment of jars containing creams or gels, a shaving brush, a loofah sponge, and a tortoiseshell handled hairbrush with three wavy silver hairs entwined in its genuine boar and nylon bristles. The scene resembles a stage set for some future audience come to witness a drama whose last act may be already over.

He removes the childproof cap from one of the pill bottles

and empties half its contents onto the bathroom counter, orange and white capsules that roll about together playfully before they come to rest. Separating the two halves of a capsule, he pours out the tiny orange pellets housed inside, retrieving some with a moistened fingertip that he sucks clean, rolling the remains around inside his mouth. He opens a second bottle, then a third, a fourth, and so on, spilling out what each one has to offer until the marble surface displays a dizzying array of choices: round pink tablets scored through the center, blue ones shaped like footballs or like hexagons, oblongs of a whitish hue; translucent lozenges of various sizes; more glistening capsules, each half a different color (red and blue, clear bottoms with black tops, or those made up of two contrasting shades of green or yellow). The caretaker tries one of the tablets, followed moments later by a capsule. He waits, pensively savoring each like a gourmand assessing an appetizer. He is in no hurry. He scoops up a small random handful and, aided by a quick slug of the amber liquid in his glass, swallows the whole handful all at once, repeating the procedure a few times at regular intervals until at last the glass is empty and he has had his fill.

The view from Dr. Morgan's baroque king-size bed consists almost entirely of an Expressionist painting on the opposite wall some eight feet tall and ten feet wide, depicting not only the bed itself with its voluptuous nest of floral pillows, but its two original occupants, the now absent Doctor and his absent Mrs. as young newlyweds, both barefoot and clad in silk pajamas, hers in a jungle pattern, his of a peculiarly acrid shade of emerald green. The Doctor reclines at the foot of the bed, propped up on an elbow with one leg cocked, while his wife leans back against the headboard behind him, her arms outstretched, cradling a pillow on either side as if she were embracing as her prized possessions an unusually adorable, if somewhat recalcitrant, pair of twins. Thanks to a deliberately skewed perspective the bed tilts downward at an impossible angle that threatens to pitch the foreground figure off the bottom of the picture even as the woman looms above him like a dark portentous angel. The portrait had been a wedding present from the artist whose career was in ascendance at the time and whom the couple had been fortunate enough to count among their closest friends. Although the picture would undoubtedly have fetched a hefty sum even then, its value had since increased tenfold as a consequence of the celebrated painter's untimely death, not to mention the more recent death of its primary subject, another well-known figure with some cachet to his name. At this point, the painting must be doomed to wind up at auction within the year, having now become worth too much for the Foundation to refrain from selling it.

By leaving intact this vestige of his former life, Dr. Morgan, for whatever improbable reason—it might have been an uncharacteristic case of nostalgia, of masochism, of mere inertia, perhaps a lingering fidelity to the wife, or even to the memory of his friend, the artist—had chosen to subject himself night after night for the better part of his adult life to a bedtime vision of a past that no longer existed and possibly never had, while the reality he actually inhabited grew to resemble it less and less. The spectacle could not have failed to disturb his sleep and infect his dreams. When he awoke, there it would be again, confronting him with its fraudulent mirror image of his existence. Every day bit by bit the chasm widened until the actual subject of the picture finally abandoned the field, leaving it to the triumph of the painter's version of what used to be.

In anticipation of visitors, the bedroom—like the rest of the residential quarters on the third floor—had been enhanced by a few carefully chosen props to perpetrate the illusion of a life still lived. They included, among several other subtler touches, a copy of *Stuff*, a well-thumbed first edition, which lay open on the nightstand, displaying, for the benefit of those who ultimately never came, the book's final chapter heading, "The Wisdom of Things."

The caretaker, swaying a little, stood transfixed beside the enormous empty bed awaiting him with its endless softly undulating white comforter. He eased himself out of Dr. Morgan's crushed, contorted slippers, which had by this time permanently transferred their allegiance to the alien feet, and took up the book, inserting two fingers between pages to keep from losing his place. Now at last, wearing nothing but the reading glasses, he slowly climbed onto the bed where the great man had intended, but failed, to die, laid his head back upon a depression in a pillow and, insinuating his angular frame into the vestigial contours of the mattress's illustrious former occupant, rested the open book face down like a tent pitched on the barren landscape of his naked chest, clasped his hands over the spine, and waited for sleep.

We too must wait. Is it possible that—while he lingers in the vast, uncharted region between here and elsewhere, between now and nevermore, between himself, the Other, and no one at all—some inchoate form of consciousness persists to helplessly record, with no interpretation, the most ephemeral of sensations—not pain, too late for that, not pleasure—maybe just the pure phenomenon of air drifting over unprotected flesh and moving on; or the celestial vision of brightly colored flashing lights emanating from somewhere deep inside his eyes as they regurgitate the light they once absorbed, expunging what they'd seen. We can only speculate. Whose heavy eyelids close the eyes and seal them shut? Whose lips draw breath? Whose formidable chest dictates the halting rhythm of the ribcage in its rise and fall? Perhaps some sort of mangled history assails him with scraps of places he had been or longed to go, with someone's guilty secrets—or are they now his own?—in which a wife whom he had never really known and never married, the wife of another man's made-up story, ministered to invisible wounds about his person and healed them. But this is only fiction. It cannot touch him anymore or make its pitiful improvements on his plot. Mind the barrier. Touching is forbidden. Inside a mind a door is slowly closing, although it makes no sound. Consciousness, that old incessant narrator, falls silent. The privacy he craves envelops him. There is at last nothing left for anyone to know—not even the omniscient—only the exquisite neutrality of silence.